BLOOD SHIELD

Life Everlasting

GLORIA FERRIS

GENRE: Young Adult/Contemporary Fantasy

Copyright © Gloria Ferris 2020 Blood Shield

ISBN: 978-1-7753392-1-2

Editor: Donna J. Warner
Cover Design: Infinite Pathways
Cover Images: © Can Stock Photos
Interior Design: Curiosity Press

Written in Canadian English.

For Dante and Talia

Keep on Imagining!

CHAPTER 1

LENNON LEANED AGAINST A LOCKER and used his enhanced eyesight to scan a list of names pinned to the bulletin board. Ignoring the dozens of kids milling around in the hall, he searched the list for the fifth time this week, hoping his appointment with the dentist had changed.

Nope, he was scheduled to have his fangs filed down today at 4 p.m. A glance at the clock over the exit door confirmed he had 45 minutes to get to Dr. Clemens' office on McKenzie Street.

Maybe he would blow off this appointment. What could they do? Except, he would end up being the only kid at Victoria High with fangs and, one way or another, the authorities wouldn't let that go for long. His case worker would nab him, take him to the dentist, and then force him into another foster home.

New plan. He could phone the dentist's office and re-schedule. Maybe next month. With no cell phone of his own, he'd have to go to the office and borrow their land line. He memorized Dr. Clemens' number from the list and turned towards the office.

Before he took a single step, a shout echoed down the hall from the principal's office. Lennon muted his super hearing but not in time to stop his ears from ringing.

The all-seeing, all-knowing Mr. Langster barrelled through the throng of students. He held the exit door open to the January air, his bushy, light hair framing his face like a lion's mane. "Okay, let's move out of the halls. Those with dental appointments, no excuses, get it over with so you can enjoy the weekend. Anyone still in the building 30 seconds from now can come with me to detention hall. Move, people!"

Mr. Langster didn't want to stay late on a Friday afternoon any more than the students, but no one planned to call his bluff. In less than the allotted time, the main hall had emptied. Lennon was one of the last out ...

And came face to face with Ashley, Jane, and Crystal. Crap! He was sure he'd given them the slip after last period.

"We're here to take you to your appointment," Ashley announced. She shook her blonde ponytail and reached for the tube of shiny stuff she covered her lips with about a hundred times a day. As usual, Lennon couldn't help watching the entire performance.

With the tube returned to the pocket of her jeans, she jerked her head towards the exit. "Let's go."

"Well, thanks, but I can manage. I know where the dentist's office is." No way were these three stalkers going with him.

CHAPTER 2

JANE PAGED THROUGH A TATTERED home decorating magazine, then threw it back on the faux-wood coffee table. She touched the top of her short red hair to make sure the gel was holding her spikes upright. All good. "It's been an hour. How long does it take to grind down a couple of eyeteeth?"

The three girls glanced uneasily at the door leading into the torture chamber. No screaming, only a deathly silence.

The skull beads on Crystal's black dreadlocks clacked as she turned back to her friends. "Maybe the dentist has to pull out Lennon's fangs. Then he'll have to get implants."

Ashley stood up and stared across the waiting room at a guy who was eyeing her up and down, the tips of his fangs peeping from between his lips. Really gross. He caught her glare and looked away. She paced between the rows of dingy, plastic chairs. "He'll be out any minute."

Jane put words to the thoughts running through Ashley's mind. "Why are we even here? More to the point, why do we bother with Lennon? It's obvious he doesn't appreciate our friendship. He runs the other way every time he sees us coming."

"Don't know," Ashley admitted. It was a question she'd been asking herself ever since the LM43 virus had been eradicated from Vancouver Island last fall. One simple inoculation had cured the afflicted and protected the general population. The ones who caught and survived the virus, like Lennon, were left with elongated canine teeth. Dentists had taken care of the adults first and, now, those eighteen and younger were undergoing filing or extractions, whichever option was deemed appropriate. Hard to believe the plague thing had been over for three months.

Ashley had been feeling responsible for Lennon's safety and wellbeing ever since the four of them had stood shoulder to shoulder, fighting the virus-enhanced outlaw biker gang that had ensnared Lennon and tried to force him to kill to become one of them. What the heck? She was sixteen, not thirty. Why should she feel so protective of a guy who obviously didn't want her anywhere near him?

A balding man in a short, white coat emerged from the door of doom and looked around his packed waiting room. Large ears stuck out at almost right angles to his head. Ashley strode over to him.

"Are you Dr. Clemens? Is Lennon done?"

The dentist's dark-eyed gaze landed on her face. His fingers pulled down on his upper lip like he was trying to cover his teeth. Maybe he used to have fangs, too. "Ah, yes, I am. Lennon is ready. Are you here to accompany him home?"

"Um, I guess. Does he need help?"

"Well, he came in a bit nervous, so we gave him a sedative. It hit him pretty hard, I'm afraid. He'll need someone to make sure he gets home and into bed. He'll be fine in a few hours."

Ashley looked around at her friends. They nodded agreement, and she turned back to the dentist. "We'll make sure he's okay."

"I'll go get him." With a last glance around the room at the fanged kids waiting their turns, he vanished into the treatment area.

By the time Ashley and her friends shrugged into their backpacks, Dr. Clemens returned, leading Lennon by the arm.

"Hey, you," the dentist shouted at a guy who was making for the door. "Get back here."

He turned to the girls. "We get a lot of runners," he explained. "Don't know why." Addressing the room of wide-eyed kids, he announced, "Nothing to it. Over in a minute and doesn't hurt a bit." Nobody believed him and even some of the parents looked traumatized.

Lennon swayed in the dentist's grip. "I'm done," he announced, staring at the ceiling. His focus made Ashley look up too, finding nothing more exciting than a light fixture with a few dead insects visible through the translucent glass. This whole place was gross.

Dr. Clemens let go of Lennon's arm and clapped him on the back. "Good boy. Show your friends your new smile."

When Lennon merely blinked at him, Dr. Clemens lifted Lennon's top lip, revealing the eyeteeth that could no longer be termed fangs. "Nice teeth, son. Never seen a set so straight without orthodontic assistance."

He surveyed the girls. "You three have perfect teeth as well. Bet you all had braces, though. Right?"

Ashley, who still wore a retainer at night, looked away from the dentist's scrutiny. "Are there any special instructions for Lennon, sir?"

"None required. Just make sure he gets home safely and sleeps it off. Hope he lives close by. Are you on foot? Yes? Excellent. A refreshing walk will do him good." After another slap on the back, Dr. Clemens gave Lennon a light shove towards the girls and called out to the others in the waiting room, "Next up, Amanda. Come right this way, young lady. Nothing to fear. It will be over before you know it. No, you can't bring your friends."

Ashley seized one of Lennon's arms, and Jane grabbed the other. Crystal scooped up his backpack, and the four teens took the elevator down to street level.

CHAPTER 3

OUTSIDE THE MEDICAL BUILDING, ASHLEY asked Lennon, "Okay, where do you live? We'll walk or take the bus, depending how far it is."

Lennon gave her a bewildered look and ran his tongue over his top teeth as though searching for something. He was drooling a bit, too.

The temperature had risen several degrees, hovering just above zero. A damp wind scattered fallen leaves and discarded wrappers against the building. Wisps of icy-cold fog floated toward them from the harbour. The mist was punctured by lights from passing vehicles and a few shop windows. Ashley pulled a toque over her ears and experienced an unwelcomed pang as she noticed Lennon shivering in his worn, leather jacket. He had no scarf, hat, or gloves. She gave his elbow a shake. "Come on, it's cold out here. Your address?"

"Thangz you, but I'm okay. Know where I live. Get home on my own. Thangz you, goodbye," he mumbled, heading for the curb. Two more steps and he'd be in the street.

"Don't think so," Ashley countered, cutting off his escape and herding him closer to the building. "Do you want us to call your foster parents? They could come pick you up." Why wasn't one of them here to help him through the whole de-fanging thing?

Lennon pulled his arm free. "Nope!" He wiped the escaping drool off his chin with his sleeve.

"Did they freeze your gums?" Crystal asked, pulling a tissue from her pocket and dabbing Lennon's face.

He poked at his top lip. "Numb. Won't work." True enough. When he spoke, his lip didn't move.

"Gee-zuz." Ashley's patience was long gone. "Tell me your address right now."

Lennon headed for the alley between two buildings. "Need to zzz-leep. For one minute."

The girls followed him. Ashley leaned him against the brick wall and gave him a shake. He was four inches taller, but he sagged in her grip. She let go, and Lennon slid down the wall until he sat on the refuse-laden concrete, legs splayed. He leaned his head back and closed his eyes.

Ashley barely restrained herself from giving him a vicious kick. Friday, already evening, and she had stuff to do. Manicure, hair trim, and two hours of defence training. She had a date tomorrow night with Devon, captain of the swim team. First date in five months. No time for this shit.

She kneeled beside Lennon and gave his face a light slap. Well, maybe not so light. "Get up. You can't sleep in here."

Between the three of them, they lifted him to his feet and steered him out of the alley. Dropping him onto a sidewalk bench, Ashley put her nose inches from his and enunciated very clearly, "There is a police officer across the street, giving us the eye. Do you want me to wave him over and ask for help getting you home? How about it? A nice ride in a warm cruiser." Kind of a lie. The scraps of fog had changed to a blanket, and she couldn't see the white line in the middle of the street, let alone the other side.

Lennon bounded up so fast, the top of his head bumped her chin and knocked her back on her heels. "No, thangz you! Just let me zzz-leep."

"Tell us where you live and you can sleep there. Last chance." Ashley rubbed her chin and resisted the temptation to smack Lennon across the back of his head.

"Alright." He sagged to the bench again and mumbled something.

"Can't hear you." Ashley got her phone out and texted the spa to cancel her appointment. In three hours she had to be at the training studio. That better be enough time to get this joker home and settled with whoever was his keeper these days.

"3300 Laurentian Drive. Ok?" He closed his eyes again.

Jane looked up from her phone. "That can't be right. He gave us the address of St. Swithin's Hospital."

"Maybe he lives on the psychiatric floor," Crystal suggested, then giggled.

Lennon struggled to his feet. "Going home to zzz-leep. Thangz you. See you ... See you ..." He lurched toward the nearest intersection where the red traffic light faded in and out of sight as the fog tendrils shifted.

Exasperated, Ashley hurried after him. Jane rolled her eyes and followed more slowly, leaving Crystal to pick up Lennon's pack from the bench and drag it along the sidewalk beside her.

Ashley stayed a few paces behind Lennon. When Crystal and Jane caught up, she said, "Don't look around. Okay, you can look, but don't be obvious. Can you make out any movement across the street? I think it's a person darting in and out of alleys but keeping up with us."

Crystal looked over her right shoulder, peeking through the dark dreadlocks before saying, "Yup, see him. Perv?"

Jane reached up to pluck at her spikes, glancing at the other side of the street. "All I can see is someone with a puffy jacket with the hood up. I think it's a guy but hard to tell in this fog."

Lennon staggered onward, in the direction of the hospital several blocks north.

Ashley whispered to her friends. "We'll just follow Lennon, see where he goes. Once we're sure he's home safe, we'll leave. Jane, stay at the end and keep that creeper in sight. It doesn't matter if he notices you looking. Maybe he'll just go away. Crys, could you pick up that pack? You're going to wear a hole in it, and I doubt Lennon has the coin for a new one."

"These things weigh a ton," Crystal griped. "The bikers are dead or in jail. Why do we need to keep dragging weapons around with us?"

"I've lost sight of the creeper," Jane announced, ignoring Crystal. "Maybe he's given up, or he could be two feet away. Who can tell?"

Shivers of unease ran up Ashley's spine. Something was way off. "Stay alert."

CHAPTER 4

"LENNON CAN'T LIVE AT ST. Swithin's." Crystal hefted the second backpack onto her free shoulder. "Most of it's abandoned. The front wing is used as a walk-in clinic, but that's it."

No one answered her as they trudged along the desolate streets.

"Park," Lennon called out. He made a hard right turn into a deserted playground.

The swings had been removed for the winter, and the rest of the play equipment turned the park into an obstacle course. Ashley bumped into a metal climber before tumbling over a crawl tube and landing on the wet ground. This was total negligence. Didn't the parks people know about rubber ground covers?

The cold mist distorted sound, and Ashley couldn't tell exactly where her friends were, but she heard their nearby grunts of pain as they either fell over a kid-sized apparatus or smacked against inflexible poles. Lennon disappeared from her view, although he could be three feet away, snoring on the teeter-totter.

A line of pine trees rose out of the fog like skeletal fingers. An edgy prickle resonated in her bones. Lennon may have headed through the trees. He retained the enhanced senses from the virus, the side effects that other victims lost when they received the curative vaccine. Meaning, if he wasn't wasted on tranquilizers, he could find his way home blindfolded with earplugs in and a fifty-pound weight tied to each leg. He wasn't aware she knew.

Ashley stood up, bracing herself against … something. A slide, maybe. "You guys, follow my voice. Lennon gave us the slip."

A hand clutched at her arm, and Jane's disembodied face popped up through the whiteness. "How about we let just let him go? We'll never find him in this mess."

Crystal's head appeared beside Jane's. "It'll be a miracle if we get back to the street ourselves. Ever notice how fog makes you lose your sense of direction?"

"We can't let Lennon wander around by himself while he's sedated. He could fall asleep and die of hypothermia …" Ashley never got to finish her sentence.

A black form hurtled out of the white void. Before the girls could reach for their weapons or even raise a defensive arm, the figure drove down through the middle of the three friends, knocking them aside.

Ashley fell to the ground and scuttled under a roundabout. Fumbling in her backpack, she located her dagger and leaped back out. First Jane, then Crystal, bounced up beside her, weapons in their hands.

"Where'd it go?" Crystal whispered, waving her hammer.

"And, what was it?" Jane raised her hatchet and peered through the swirling haze.

"Perimeter defence," Ashley ordered. "It moves like some kind of ninja."

They formed a circle, backs together, facing out, weapons held chest high in readiness.

"This is like old times," Crystal joked. "Except we don't have a clue who the enemy is."

The mist cleared momentarily, allowing Ashley to see the dark figure leaping around like an athletic ghost. "He's about thirty metres in front of us, near the treeline. I think he's after Lennon, not us. There's some kind of weapon in his hand."

Now the girls stood side by side, facing the forest. The fog closed in and reduced their visibility to less than six inches. Ashley was aware that the threat could be upon them before they had a chance to raise their weapons.

The skin on her neck prickled double time. "I don't like standing in the open where we can't see ..."

In her peripheral vision, she caught a glimpse of a padded shoulder as it came up from behind, shoving through the centre of their lineup. Ashley hooked her arm over a climbing bar to prevent another fall to the ground. By the sounds of her friends' grunts, they weren't as lucky.

Through a parting in the vapour, Ashley watched Padded Jacket run unerringly at Ninja Boy. The echoes of hand to hand fighting filled the playground as the two figures blocked blows and kicked at each other. Ashley's eyes failed to follow the bursts of movement and she lost track of who was who. Transfixed, she ignored her friends' pleas to escape from the battlefield.

With the mist cutting in and out, she could only discern legs and arms flying in a flurry of blocks, punches, and kicks. She had barely learned the front kick and the knee strike, and these combatants were performing complicated moves. She saw Ninja Boy throw a flying side kick, only to be knocked to the ground by a hopping front kick delivered by Padded Jacket. Gee-zuz, she wished she could fight like this.

One second the fight appeared to be accelerating, the next it was over. Ninja Boy ran off in the direction of the street. Padded Jacket turned, and it seemed to Ashley that he looked straight at her before executing a slight bow and disappearing in the opposite direction from his opponent.

Beside her, Jane delved inside her backpack for her hatchet sheath and snapped it over the blade. "What the hell just happened?"

Crystal dropped her hammer into her pack and swung it over her shoulder. "The second guy with the padded jacket was the creeper who followed us from the dentist. I'm sure of it."

"Something weird is going on." Ashley didn't feel good about stowing her dagger just yet. "I didn't get the impression either of them was after us."

She peered into the clouds of fog rolling over the playground. "I think Lennon was the target."

CHAPTER 5

CRYSTAL STOOPED TO PICK UP Lennon's backpack. "He's probably at home already, and has no idea what just happened. And, I'm stuck with his stuff. What am I supposed to do with it all weekend? What if he has homework he needs to do?"

"I bet he's sleeping it off at the foot of a tree." Jane waved her hand in the direction of the woods. "And, he'll freeze to death if we don't find him. What a pain. Tell me again why we bother. Seriously, tell me."

"Good question." Ashley put her dagger back in its scabbard but left the flap of her backpack open, just in case. She spied the playground's crawl tube through the fog, touched the smooth, damp surface, and sat down.

"I'm still waiting for an answer to that question. Why do we follow Lennon around like a pack of guard dogs?" Jane pointed overhead. "Never mind. I think it's clearing up. I can see the tops of the trees."

"Guess we'll have to search over there, but stay together or we'll all get lost." Ashley checked her phone for the time. Two hours before they had to be at the training studio.

A loud *snore-snort* emanated from the crawl tube under Ashley's butt. She sprang up, automatically reaching for her dagger. The next second, her brain identified the sound. She relaxed, although she was uncomfortably aware that the seat of her jeans had soaked up the cold moisture from the surface of the tube.

Shivering, she aimed her phone into the interior of the tube. "Gee-zuz, here he is." Lennon looked peaceful enough and, for an instant, Ashley considered leaving him there. He'd probably be fine.

No, he wouldn't. "Shoot. Okay, somebody has to go inside and drag him out. Jane, you're the smallest."

Jane didn't budge from her spot a few feet away. "Lennon is bigger than all of us, and he fits. You go; he likes you best."

"Yeah, right," Ashley retorted. She looked in Crystal's direction. "Crystal?" Someday soon she had to tell Crystal her clacking beads were always a dead giveaway to her location, even when she thought she was hiding.

"Not doing it." Crystal's words came fast and final.

"Fine!" Ashley crawled into the tube, her phone light revealing Lennon's form slumped against the plastic wall. She had to punch him on the arm to wake him, but she'd been itching to do that for a while. Once he opened his eyes, she put her phone away and clutched the collar of his jacket. She dragged his limp body to the opening, inch by inch. It took forever to get him out. By the time she rolled onto the ground, Ashley was exhausted.

She swept her light over him and found he was fast asleep again, one cheek flat against the sodden, beaten grass. Observing something stuck to the back of his jacket, Ashley pulled off a 3inch, light brown hair. She made a face and tossed it down. Definitely not from the bald dentist. She hefted Lennon to his feet. Without a word, he stumbled towards the trees. This time, Ashley and her friends followed closely until they emerged onto the hospital street.

Lennon stopped when he reached an empty parking lot behind the abandoned hospital. Night had fallen and a few remaining streetlamps bathed the cracked asphalt in a dim, yellow light. A camera mounted on a pole pointed its lens at the grey stones of the hospital walls. The lower floors were eerily veiled in puffs of ghostly vapour.

"I don't think we're being followed," Jane said. "I've been watching and can't see anything moving."

The tingly feeling had disappeared from Ashley's skin. "I agree. We're alone here."

Lennon flattened his body against the wall and side-stepped along the bricks as though avoiding the eye of the camera which probably hadn't worked since the Biebs was a baby. When he reached the corner, he slid to his hands and knees, disappearing from sight.

Maybe the camera did work. Ashley drew the hood of her coat over her toque and pulled up the zipper as far as it would go. Jane and Crystal followed Ashley, hugging the wall, keeping their faces turned away from the camera. Ashley rounded the corner and slammed her toe into a rock-hard surface.

Biting back a screech of pain, Ashley blinked a few times until her night vision kicked in. "There's a huge rock here. Anybody got a freaking flashlight?" She didn't want to take the chance of dropping her phone.

Jane, at the back of the line, handed a flashlight to Crystal, who passed it to Ashley. Dimming the beam with her free hand, Ashley shone it at the boulder.

CHAPTER 6

WHAT THE HELL? ASHLEY SWEPT the light in a circle. "There's a gap here, then a bunch more ginormous rocks."

"Why would Lennon come through here?" Crystal asked. "Can you see anything on the other side, Ash?"

"There's some stairs leading down to a small landing. I'm going down to see if there's any sign of Lennon. Wait here."

As Ashley lifted one foot to descend, the weight of both her friends pressing against her back knocked her off-balance.

She wobbled at the edge, and tried to fling her body back, but Crystal stood too close. Both girls fell, landing at the bottom in a tangle of limbs. With the weight of her friend on top of her, Ashley's face pressed painfully against the frigid surface.

"Get ... off ... me," Ashley croaked. She had a dagger in her backpack. That thing could kill her if it pierced a lung, or some other major organ. Well, okay, it was sheathed, but still.

Crystal got to her knees and, by the sound of her beads tapping together, was shaking her head to clear it. Using Crystal as a prop, Ashley got to her feet.

Amazingly, the flashlight lens hadn't shattered. The beam spotlighted a concrete pad no more than four feet square. Above their heads, a ring of landscaping boulders surrounded the stairway.

"So, no Lennon, right?" Jane called down. She took the steps two at a time to land beside her friends.

"Thanks for your concern, Jane. We're fine in case you were wondering." Ashley touched her cheek which stung like fight night at a murder hornet convention.

"I count eight steps," Jane announced. "You guys hit every one."

Ashley aimed the beam at the wall.

"Wow, look at that," Crystal said. "That door looks like it's made of industrial metal. And, there's no handle. Don't think we're meant to be down here."

Ashley noticed something else interesting. Or maybe she had a concussion. She turned off the flashlight and let the darkness enclose them. "See that?"

A thin rim of light surrounded the door. It hadn't been tightly closed. Ashley ripped off her mitt with her teeth and pried at the edge of the door. The cold steel made her fingers ache and destroyed the last of her manicure. Now she had to go all weekend with ragged nails.

The steel door finally yielded enough to get her shoulder through. She shoved it wider and slid through the opening.

What was this place? A first glance around the space didn't tell her much. Crystal edged her aside, and she sensed Jane tumble through the doorway.

An old boiler room, or something? Huge, about twenty metres by fifteen. Lots of pipes and groaning vents covered the ceiling. And ... What was this?

Lennon, still wearing his leather jacket, was asleep on a rusted, metal bed in one corner. His mouth hung open and soft snores erupted. The room was toasty warm. On the floor beside the bed, a heap of tattered blankets lay bunched up like a nest.

Jane bumped Ashley's elbow. She pointed to the occupant of an oversized rocking chair placed strategically under a heating vent. "Uh, any idea what that is?"

CHAPTER 7

ASHLEY FOLLOWED THE PATH OF Crystal's finger. Clapping her hand over her mouth to stifle the screech that bubbled up, she fumbled for the dagger in her pack. Jane produced her machete, and a steel hammer materialized in Crystal's hand. They assumed a fighting stance and stared at the creature in the chair.

It stopped rocking and jumped up, backing against the wall. The thing was five feet tall and almost as wide with long, light-brown hair covering its body and face. Making a loud mewling noise like a giant kitten, it took two strides across the room to the bed, bounding over Lennon's body to curl up behind him. Round, yellow eyes rimmed in black stared back at the girls.

"Maybe a humongous monkey?" Crystal suggested, backing towards the door.

"Kinda looks like Chewbacca." Jane lowered the

machete an inch. "Except it's smaller and lighter in colour."

Ashley walked slowly to the bed, dagger still clutched in her right fist, tip pointed upwards. This must be the source of the hair she found on Lennon's jacket. Without taking her eyes off the creature, she poked a finger into Lennon's chest. "Hey, wake up. You have a lot of explaining to do."

Lennon ran his tongue over his upper lip. Apparently satisfied it was still there, he rolled over towards the animal, fumbling for one of its immense paws. "Hi, Hank. I'm home, buddy."

The creature's stare moved back and forth between Ashley and the other girls standing in front of the door. Ashley very carefully reached out to Lennon. This time, she dug her fingers into the back of his neck and squeezed. He yelped and shot straight up on the bed.

Catching sight of his visitors, he pressed against the hairy animal that wrapped its arms protectively around him.

"How did you get in here?" He glared at Ashley.

"We followed you. And, you left your door open a crack. Anybody could just walk in." Why was she explaining herself to Lennon and his pet-whatever-the-hell-this-thing-was?

"Okay, so now you know where I live. You can leave and take your weapons with you."

Ashley lowered the dagger but didn't move back. "Not without some answers, starting with that *thing.*

What is Hank and where did you get him?"

Lennon's brain wasn't working right but his gut told him he'd better straighten out fast or he'd be in big trouble. Why he cared what these girls thought of him wasn't the issue. No matter how hard he tried to blow them off, they wouldn't leave him alone. Just because they fought side by side for their lives a few months ago, it didn't mean they were all best friends. He was grateful for their help in making his transition back to high school life easier, but he had changed. He was stronger and he was going to make it clear once and for all that they should stop stalking him and bossing him around.

"Um, Hank?" Lennon flinched even before Ashley poked him again with her finger, this time in the arm.

"Yes. Your hairy friend, here." Ashley's finger poised for another strike.

Lennon scrambled off the bed, his legs buckling beneath him. That sedative the dentist gave him shouldn't have affected him. It must have been a whopper of a dose, meant for an elephant. He crawled to the rocking chair, his head swimming, before checking his eyeteeth with his tongue. Just dull points, the way eyeteeth were supposed to feel.

In a way, he was going to miss his fangs.

Hank jumped from the bed and squatted in front of Lennon, leaning against his legs. Ashley needed to quit waving that dagger around and put it away. She was scaring Hank. Lennon patted his new friend's trembling shoulder and murmured, "It's okay, man. They won't hurt you."

Ashley checked her phone with her free hand like she had some important place to be. "Your animal, Lennon? What is it?"

"Hank is not an animal. I think he's a Sasquatch. Just a kid." He was almost sure that Hank was more human than animal.

"Ha. Sasquatches aren't real." Ashley approached, but stayed at arm's length. Like that would help if Hank decided she was an enemy and jumped her. Lennon squeezed Hank's shoulder to keep him calm, not that Hank had ever shown signs of aggression.

"A few months ago, we thought there were no such things as fangs and blood-drinkers, and super strength. We all know different, now."

"He's got a point, Ash." Jane moved up slowly to stand beside Ashley. "Things are taking a turn for the weird again."

Crystal stayed by the door, one hand clutching her stupid hammer, like she was Thor or something, except she wasn't blond, or a god. "Our reality has changed, that's for sure. A virus that enhances strength and turns eyeteeth into fangs? We didn't think all that was possible a few months ago. Why not Sasquatches?"

Ashley glanced around at her, then turned back and rolled her eyes. "Okay, I'll bite. Lennon, why do you think Hank is a Sasquatch? He could be some kind of gorilla. He's big and brown and hairy. True, he has longer legs and shorter arms, and a flatter forehead. Maybe he's the result of a lab accident. That, I'd believe."

Lennon's head was starting to clear. The numbness in his lip had all but disappeared, replaced by itchy-tingling. He waited until Ashley wound down before answering. "He followed me home so I kept him."

CHAPTER 8

"WHEN, AND FROM WHERE?" THE tone of Ashley's voice made her disbelief obvious, even without the accompanying eye roll.

"Last Sunday. I was out by the Spirit Railway Junction. Sometimes, I find neat things dropped beside the tracks and between the ties. Hank just walked out of the bush. He looked lost and hungry, so I brought him home until I could take him back into the forest and find where he came from. I think he's about our age, maybe a lot younger. He doesn't seem too good at looking after himself."

Ashley clapped her hands over her temples and pressed, while Jane muttered, "Weird," over and over. Crystal stayed near the door, her almond-shaped eyes darting around the room like she expected a dozen more Sasquatches to leap from the shadowed corners.

Lennon yawned and looked at the three girls. "So, I'm fine. Thanks for helping me get home." Not really, but they had good intentions. No point being rude. "You can go home now. It's Friday night. I'm sure you have stuff to do."

"Okay, we'll drop the subject of Hank for now," Ashley responded, not moving. "A couple other things, though. First, you live in a creepy, old building. What happened to your foster family? Does your case worker know where you are?"

"About that." He better shut this down right now. "My foster family got a new kid while I was living with the bikers and they don't want me back but we're pretending I'm still there. The Wilsons are still getting paid for me so we came to an agreement. They give me a hundred bucks a month and when the case worker plans a visit, Mrs. Wilson calls me, and I go over there and we pretend everything is good with me. Next year, I'm eligible for a group home, and I might consider that. So, that's why I'm here."

Jane gave him one of her flinty-eyed looks. "Uh, you don't have a phone. How do the Wilsons let you know when your case worker is coming?"

"They call the school and leave a message for me to call them."

Ashley didn't look satisfied. She reached up to tighten her blonde ponytail. Her ice blue eyes bore into the side of his throat, and he pulled up his collar protectively in case she squeezed his neck again.

He should have known she wouldn't stop badgering him.

"Next up, and I know you missed the whole thing because you were sleeping in a crawl tube, but why did one man follow us from the dental office, then get in a fight with another man in the park? They weren't after us. Is there a reason why a couple of hand-to-hand experts are looking for you?"

"You're joking, right?" He looked at their solemn expressions and realized Ashley was telling the truth. "I haven't a clue. Nobody is after me." Not entirely true. Someone had been following him for a while, but no reason for the girls to know. They'd stick to him like Velcro.

Ashley moved on relentlessly to another point. "Why did the dentist give you a sedative? You didn't seem nervous when you went in, and it's not like filing down a tooth is life-bending. And ..."

He braced himself as she pulled his collar away from his skin, "... you have a needle hole in your neck."

CHAPTER 9

LENNON RUBBED THE SORE LUMP on his neck and thought for a moment. "Yeah, now that you mention it, the dentist said he was going to give me something to relax me, then jabbed me in the neck. Don't know why; he said my fangs weren't especially long. I wasn't afraid, either." Even stranger, the injection site should have healed already. But he wasn't ready to tell Ashley that he hadn't lost his superhuman abilities including accelerated healing. The vaccine should have taken care of all that. Maybe he was just slower to recover? At least he no longer craved blood.

Hank got up from the floor and bent his neck toward Ashley, close enough to lay his head on her shoulder but not quite touching. That was his friendly gesture, like he wanted to be buddies, but Ashley didn't get it. She moved back a few feet.

"Then what? You were in there for over an hour. I know it doesn't take that long to file down two eyeteeth." Ashley pulled out the silver tube from the pocket of her jeans and coated her lips with shiny stuff, again. "What happened and what did he say?"

Lennon watched until she put the tube back in her pocket. Fact was, he couldn't remember much of his dentist`s visit, not after the jab in the neck, anyway.

"Well, he must have filed my fangs. They're gone." Lennon touched his polished eyeteeth with the tip of his tongue. "He could have left them a bit pointier."

Crystal took a step forward but kept her hammer in sight. "Dentists always yammer at you when your mouth is full of fingers and sucky tubes."

"Think," Ashley snapped. "What did he say?"

Lennon's brain was still muddled. "I know what you're getting at. Did he ask me if my senses are still enhanced, or if I still have super strength and speed? Well, he might have clued into something when he dropped a sharp pick, and I grabbed it before it hit the floor." Oops.

"You're saying he stabbed you with a tranquilizer after you demonstrated you didn't lose your abilities after the vaccine?" Ashley's eyebrows rose ceiling-ward, like she was dealing with an idiot – like old times, this was. She didn't sound surprised, though.

Crystal's head clackity-clacked back and forth between Lennon and Ashley. "What. You mean you still have all your super powers like before you got the vaccine? Did you know that, Ash?"

"She knew," Lennon spoke before Ashley could deny it.

"I'm observant," Ashley said.

Jane whooped, startling Hank into clutching Lennon's arm. "And, the weird continues." She reached over and patted Hank's paw — hand — reassuringly. "Sorry, Hank." When Hank didn't pull away, Jane closed her fingers over his. Hank blinked his golden eyes and made a purring, happy sound.

Ashley checked her phone screen again. "We have fifty minutes to get to taekwondo class. Come on, Lennon, think harder. What did you tell the dentist?"

"I don't remember anything that happened after he stabbed me, so I could have told him anything ..."

"... or everything," Ashley finished his sentence for him, an annoying habit which kind of got on his nerves, like she knew what he was going to say before he even said it.

Giving Lennon a pissy look, Ashley said, "Too many strange things have happened today. Lennon gets zapped senseless for a minor procedure that should have taken twenty minutes tops but takes over an hour; two people follow us from the building but don't approach; there's a battle in the playground — in the fog — but neither guy is after us."

Crystal finally stowed her hammer, either because her arm gave out, or she was re-assured by Jane and

Hank holding hands. "It all has to be connected."

"Don't forget Hank," Jane leaned against the bed and showed Hank how to swipe the screen on her phone to change the photos.

"Not sure Hank is connected to the rest," Ashley responded. "We'll run back to the dental building where there are lights and other people. I'll call a taxi to pick us up there. We can still make our class if we leave now."

She turned back to Lennon. "Tomorrow is Saturday. We'll meet up and talk more about tonight. Maybe figure it out."

"Can't," Lennon told her decisively. "Tomorrow, I'm taking Hank back to the forest. His family is probably looking for him. Once we get in deep enough, they should come for him, or he'll know his way home."

"What's the hurry?" Jane asked. "Hank is friendly and he's company for you." By this time, she was sitting on the edge of the bed beside Hank, crowding Lennon against the rusty metal rails of the headboard.

"He eats more than five grown men. I've been spending a lot of time dumpster-diving behind restaurants to get him enough vegetables and fruit. He needs to get back to his family. They'll be worried about him." Hank had only been with him a few days, but Lennon's heart ached, knowing Hank would soon be gone.

"How do you figure on getting deep enough into the forest for his family to find him?" Ashley asked.

"Then, you'll probably get lost trying to get home. If you don't show up at school on Monday, there goes your whole foster family fairy tale. Everybody is busted. The Wilsons never get to foster any more kids, and you go to a new home."

Lennon hunched his shoulders. "I talked to some of the guys that work at the switchyard. I found out a train goes into the interior to drop off water and supplies for a logging company. It goes in and out at the same times, every day except Sundays. One engine, one freight car — and it isn't full. They load up the night before and head out early the next morning. Hank and I are going to get there tonight and climb in. I figure Hank will sense when we're close to his home, and we can jump off. Because of the winding track around all the trees, the train goes super slow."

A heartbeat later, Ashley announced, "We're going with you."

Nope. No. No. No. "Uh, not necessary, Ashley, but thanks for the offer. I'll be gone overnight." He struggled for a way to change her mind. "No cell reception. No bathrooms, no Starbucks, no showers ..."

Jane faced Ashley. "Are you nuts? We can't do that."

Crystal's head swivelled back and forth between her friends. "You're kidding, right? It's freezing in the woods this time of year. What will we tell our parents?"

As if that was a problem for Ashley. "We'll dress warm, and our plan is the usual. I'm staying over with Crystal. Crystal is at Jane's and Jane is at my house. We'll tell our parents we'll be hiking and could be out of tower range at times. Problem solved. We'll make our self-defence class tonight, go home and gear up, and meet Lennon and Hank at the switchyard. Everybody got it?"

Everybody did, including Lennon, after she gave him a hard stare. He already knew this was not going to end well.

CHAPTER 10

THEY MADE THEIR TAEKWONDO CLASS with minutes to spare. Ashley had trouble keeping her mind on the exercises and, by the way Crystal and Jane fumbled the basic techniques, they were thinking about a cold night in the bushes and an even colder ride in a freight train. After that, Ashley had no idea what they would encounter.

The owner of the martial arts school, Master Peter Li, reserved Friday night class for female beginners. Most of the other students were a couple of years younger than Ashley and her friends. One kid looked about 12.

When he figured they were ready, Master Li moved students into a mixed class so females got a taste of fighting opponents bigger and stronger. By the looks he gave Ashley, Jane and Crystal in the back row, they weren't going to be moved up any time soon. Master led them through the final form — a sequence of fight moves against an imaginary opponent. But no matter how hard Ashley tried to concentrate on her breathing, her mind wandered back to Ninja Boy and Padded Jacket.

Would she ever be able to fight like them? Maybe if she'd started training when she was four, and not three months ago after their battle with the virus-enhanced bikers. The self-defence class for women that they took in Grade 9 taught them how to knee an attacker in the groin and stomp on wrists and ankles but that wasn't going to be enough for what they would face in the future. Ashley knew that and it bugged her that she didn't know why she knew. It wasn't like she was psychic.

Class ended and the group dispersed. Crystal caught up with Master before he disappeared into his office at the back of the training floor. Master and Crystal were related, second cousins, or maybe third, Ashley could never remember. She followed Crystal and stood back as Crystal recounted their run-in with the two martial arts experts in the park.

"It wasn't just taekwondo, either," Crystal explained. "They moved so fast, it was hard to see, and I'm sure I saw some Krav Maga. Those guys meant business."

By the crinkles around his eyes, Master was dad-age, but he didn't have a dad bod. He looked at the three girls, one after the other, and didn't speak for some time. Ashley was sure he was going to demote them to his pre-teen class.

To break the silence, Ashley blurted out, "Can you teach us to fight with weapons? There's a lot of weird stuff going on in our lives, and it's taking too long to learn how to deal with people that want to kill us."

Whoops. She shouldn't have said that. Why had she? Now, Master would want to know who was threatening them and why they didn't go to the police or their parents. Answer: because it was *really* weird shit and authority figures wouldn't believe them.

Master didn't say whether he believed them or not, simply asking, "What kind of weapons are you using?"

"Dagger," Ashley responded.

"I favour a hatchet." Jane crossed her arms and waited for their taekwondo master to laugh.

He didn't. He glanced at Crystal.

"Hammer. I'm thinking of trading up to a metal meat tenderizer. More surface area."

Master blinked at that statement. "Very resourceful, Crystal. Now, you realize that those weapons need a lot of swinging room. They're useless when the threat is up close. It's going to be many years before you master taekwondo which is good for self-defence against a regular attacker but not as useful if your opponent is using another discipline."

He looked from one face to another. "I suggest you

continue with your present lessons for now, and begin adding Krav Maga to your skills. I will hold a class for the three of you on Saturday mornings. No charge. Once I'm satisfied you can handle a more combative form of martial art, you can drop taekwondo. Krav Maga was not created as a martial art, but as a training system for Israeli soldiers and is invaluable for defensive and disarming techniques. That is what you need by the sounds of it."

Wow, great to have a relative around to give you freebies. Lennon should come, too. He couldn't fight as well as they did.

After exchanging eye locks with her friends, it looked like they were in favour of Master's offer. No more sleeping in Saturday mornings. For now, Friday night and Saturday morning were reserved for fight school.

"Thanks, Peter, I mean Master." Crystal gave her cousin a hug. "Can we start next week? We, uh, have a commitment tomorrow."

"How long before we get a black belt in Krav Maga?" Jane asked.

Master's lips lifted in a half-smile before his face recovered its usual stern expression. "If you work really hard, you can reach black belt status in about four years. After that, it takes a minimum of five years per Dan level in the black belt system. There are five Dans. It takes many, many years to become a true expert."

Gee-zuz. She'd be over 30 by then. Ashley didn't care about belt levels or whatever. She just wanted not to die if another ninja ran at her. Just because the one tonight wasn't after them, didn't mean more threatening baddies weren't out there.

"Guess we better get started — next week. Will you teach us how to fight with smaller weapons, Master?" Ashley already knew she couldn't defend herself with kicks and blocks, even punches. She preferred to wield a weapon, but he was right — daggers, hammers, and hatchets wouldn't do the job for close up encounters. She and her friends were skilled with using bows and arrows, but that wouldn't help close up any more than their present weapons. Guns were totally out. So, what did that leave?

"I can't legally teach you to fight with weapons — of any size. However, after I leave the floor, if you happen to open the box in the corner of the room behind you, and a weapon chooses you, then that may be destiny. They are to be used only to save your lives. Defensively, not offensively."

The girls bowed to the Master, and he returned the gesture. He backed away and disappeared into the gloomy shadows beyond the training floor.

They hurried to the location Master had pointed to. Ashley snatched up her phone from her backpack on the way. When she shined the light on the darkest corner, they discovered — a plastic tackle box.

"Is this a joke?" Jane grumbled. "Lures and hooks. That should scare away the evil creatures who follow us by day and haunt our dreams by night."

Ashley swept her friend's face with the light. "That was very dramatic, Jane. Thinking of trying out for Theatre Club?"

Not waiting for an answer, she turned the light on Crystal. "Master Li is your cousin, Crys. You open the box. If something jumps out, it'll land on you."

"Don't see the logic, but okay." Crystal unsnapped the closure on the plastic box, flipped the lid open, and scrambled back.

Nothing flew at them. They leaned over the objects neatly lining the two-tiered interior of the tackle box.

Ashley lifted her head. "Not impressed."

CHAPTER 11

BOTH TRAYS HELD NEAT ROWS of oblong objects from five to six inches in length.

Crystal gave one of the items a prod, then picked it up. "This one's pretty, but what is it?" It was iridescent and faintly pink, like mother of pearl. An embedded, clear crystal glowed softly at one end.

"I know!" Jane grabbed it out of Crystal's hand. "It has an on-off switch, then a deployment button ..."

She pressed down and a blade shot from the end.

"A toy switchblade?" Ashley placed her finger at the end of the two-and-a half inch blade. "Sort of sharp. I could clean my nails with it."

"It's a mini switchblade." Jane used her free hand to touch the weapons in the box, one by one.

Crystal carefully prised the pink pearl knife from Jane's fingers. "This one's mine. Peter said to go with the one that chooses us, and this little sweetie practically jumped into my hand. It even has a real crystal, totally meant for me."

"Ha!" Jane snatched up a white-handled weapon. When she deployed the blade, it was black and razor-sharp. The same length as Crystal's. "Did you see that? It buzzed in my hand when I touched it. It's a bit stiff to open but some WD40 will loosen it up."

She scooted away from the box. "What about you, Ash? Let one choose you."

"You know these are prohibited weapons in this country, right? Doesn't matter how small they are. Automatic knives are illegal. Period." Ashley's eyes were drawn to the bottom tray, but she forced herself to look at her friends.

Jane made an unflattering snorting sound. "Your dagger is prohibited; so is my hatchet and Crystal's stupid hammer simply because we intend them for defence. The bear spray canisters we carry around are prohibited unless there are bears right up in our faces. The throwing stars Lennon used in the cemetery against the bikers are prohibited ..."

"Not to mention we broke the law by torching those run-down warehouses and nearly killing a couple of bad, bad dudes." Crystal held her switchblade up to the light to watch the gemstone sparkle. "Good thing no one found out about that."

Ashley moved closer to the box, still trying to avoid looking at the bottom tray. "Ancient history. The whole archery team knows about the warehouses. Let's hope they don't ever blab or it's good-bye to my future law career."

"You sound just like the goody-goody cheerleader you used to be," Jane scoffed. "Remember, you gave up cheer to learn how to fight. Weird things happened during the freaking plague and weird things are still happening. Look at Lennon. He didn't lose his super strength or enhanced senses. So, probably other people didn't either. And, we met a Sasquatch. Seriously, the world is not the way we thought it was. Until everybody else catches up, we have to protect ourselves. A tiny switchblade doesn't seem so bad."

"Very profound words, Jane." The rational part of Ashley's mind gave way to temptation, and she reached into the dimness of the bottom tray. Her fingers closed over a knife — she couldn't make out the colour or size until it lay in the palm of her hand.

A swirl of yellows and greens glinted in the hazy light — maybe marble or enamelled metal — and cool against her skin. Not pretty like Jane's and Crystal's. She slid the switch to the on position and pressed the button. A thin blade burst from concealment.

She closed the knife and slid it into her pocket before she overthought the decision she just made. "When we're lost in the bush, eating bark and leaves, I'll have something to pick my teeth with. Come on, we have some planning and packing to do."

Crystal closed the tackle box and pushed it

against the wall. "I've always wanted to visit the Spirit Switchyard at midnight. As if. It might be more fun than summer school, though."

CHAPTER 12

AT THE EDGE OF THE switchyard where clumps of stunted pines struggled to survive, Lennon huddled next to Hank for warmth and avoided eye contact with the spectres.

Just his freaking luck he could see ghosts. He'd seen a few when he was a kid, but his mom acted like it was no big deal. She said they were just imprints left behind and that not everyone could sense or see the remnants of energy. After she abandoned him when he was ten, Lennon stopped seeing *remnants*. Then he was bitten by an outlaw biker with the LM43 virus that the World Health Organization called a mutation of the Lassa fever virus. Plague, more like it. After Lennon was cured, he kept his enhanced senses and speed, and the ghosts showed up again. Like, everywhere.

By their clothes, these scraps of energy from the departed stayed around forever. He'd seen colonists arriving at the harbour; ladies wearing fancy, huge hats with feathers; men in uniform from both the First and Second World Wars. Lennon watched them walk slowly away from their ships until they disappeared.

Last month, he'd seen a kid his own age hanging around in an alley with a Vic High School football team jacket, and his throat had two puncture marks. Lennon didn't look closely at his face, not wanting to recognize him. There were a couple dozen kids missing from school these days, victims of the virus carriers who were unable to control their blood thirst and sucked their prey dry instead of just drinking enough to infect them.

At first, he was scared of the spectres. But, while a few of them looked in his direction as though they sensed something out of time, they didn't interact with him or try and communicate. It was as if they existed on a parallel plane or something, just doing what they did when they were alive.

The group over by the tracks sat on overturned barrels and warmed their hands over a fire that burned green flames. That's how Lennon knew they were ghosts. They all looked shimmery green, their outlines wavering like they would disappear any second. They did fade away, eventually. But this lot, either hobos who rode the rails during the Great

Depression of the 1930s or workers who had built the tracks in the 1800s and died here, continued to eat out of tin cans and edge closer to the fire.

Lennon glanced at Hank, wondering if he could see them. Hank crunched down on his last head of wilted lettuce and tilted his head at Lennon's backpack, as if questioning its contents.

"That's it for now, buddy," Lennon told his friend. "No more food until we get you back into the forest."

They'd stopped off at the dumpster behind the Water Lily Chinese restaurant and scored three heads of limp lettuce, a crate of watercress, and a plastic bag of assorted chopped vegetables that were only slightly brown at the edges. Hank ate all the watercress and the chopped vegetables on the spot while Lennon kept watch and shoved the heads of lettuce and a bunch of carrots into his pack. A whistling, homeless dude had wheeled in his heaping shopping cart ready to forage through the dumpster. One look at Hank and he dragged his cart backwards out of the alley, not missing a beat in his tuneless whistle.

Lennon also packed his own food, everything he had in his home which wasn't much. A few energy bars, a package of dried cereal, and a few bottles of water. Now his stomach growled, but he knew from past experience he had to pace himself or he'd eat everything at once and end up starved tomorrow. The hundred dollars a month he got from his former foster father barely covered a haircut, school supplies, and the two-fifty a shot he spent on showers at a local gym. Then there was the laundromat, and he was saving up to buy a heavier coat from the army surplus store. Leather looked cool, but it didn't keep the chilly winter rain from running down the back of his neck.

So, food was becoming a problem. There were a few burger places near his home that sometimes threw out cooked meat after the restaurant closed. If the food smelled fresh and didn't look like someone had taken a bite, Lennon would snag it and put it into a plastic bag. If there was only a small bite out of one side, he might take it as well and cut that part off when he got home. If someone else was already rummaging through the cans, Lennon would either find another restaurant or go home empty-handed. He avoided confrontations, not daring to call attention to himself.

He squirmed with shame when he remembered the few times he had actually stolen food. Once, he had walked through a grocery store parking lot and lifted a plastic bag from a cart as a lady turned to open the back of her SUV. When he got home and looked inside, he had a dozen eggs, a package of bacon, and three boxes of mac and cheese. And, no way to cook any of it, although he had soaked the macaroni in water and sprinkled the cheese over top. Another time, he scooped up a paper sack of fast food from someone sitting on a bench in Trafalgar Square. He darted into a nearby alley and wolfed down the French fries, veggie burger, and a cola. That's when he'd seen the ghost kid from school with the puncture marks.

He needed to get a part-time job. Not that he hadn't tried. Nobody was hiring although he went around to the pizza and burger places, and other local businesses almost every day after school. Maybe now that his fangs were gone, he'd have better luck ...

Snap!

Lennon had engaged his enhanced hearing when they arrived at the switchyard. At least a hundred metres away, a foot stepped on a twig. He shoved away from Hank and leaped to his feet. Hank heard it too. The Sasquatch clambered into the lower branches of a spindly pine. A branch cracked and, before Lennon's super speed could move him out of danger, Hank dropped six feet to the ground, pinning Lennon under a hundred and fifty pounds of muscle and fur.

CHAPTER 13

SNAP!

Ashley halted and reached over her shoulder for her dagger. "Wait. Did you hear that?"

"Hear what?" Crystal whispered back. "I can't even hear crickets or grass growing in this wasteland."

"It's winter, you maniac. Crickets and grass are dead until spring." Jane kept her eyes on the ground trying not to trip over fallen branches or walk into a tree. "Why are you so paranoid, Ash? There's nothing here."

"I think I stepped in some dog poop," Crystal complained.

"Eeww." Jane pushed her way past Ashley into the lead. "Wipe your shoe off. I don't want to ride in a confined space with dog poop."

"Shh," Ashley cautioned. "I'm sure I heard

something." She ushered Crystal ahead and stood still, listening. Crystal was right. There was nothing here. But, she was sure she heard a sound, like a foot stepping on a dried piece of wood.

Jane joggled Ashley's arm to get her attention. "Maybe Lennon and Hank aren't here yet. We should hear them talking, or moving around."

Crystal leaned against a tree. "Hank and Lennon can't talk to each other. And, where is this ancient train junction we're looking for? We could be lost in the forest and never find our way out."

With dagger in hand, Ashley kept her back to her friends and strained her eyes to see any movement in the woods. "We can't walk straight through the switchyard, even when we find it. Lennon said they load the boxcar every night and leave early in the morning. We need to make sure no one is around."

"They must have a night watchman," Crystal argued. "Else, the boxcar would be robbed."

"What if they lock the boxcar after they load? We won't be able to get in and hide out." Jane sounded almost hopeful.

Ashley slid her dagger into the back holster she had found among her dad's belongings in the garage. She'd slipped it on as soon as the taxi let them out near the train terminal and had been practising, repeatedly pulling the weapon out and re-holstering it as they made their way toward the semi-abandoned switchyard. The taxi driver was reluctant to let them off, pointing out the trains had stopped running on the Island years ago. They reassured him they were doing some winter camping, indicating their bulging packs. He finally drove off, glancing at them in his side mirror, as if memorising their faces in case he was called on to identify their bodies in the morgue in the not too distant future.

Ashley shielded her phone screen with her hand and checked the GPS. "The switchyard should be east a few hundred yards. We're almost at the edge of this scrubby forest." She checked the weather app. "Full moon tonight. I guess that's why it isn't completely dark out here, even with all the cloud cover."

Jane groaned. "East? Is that left, right, straight ahead, or back the way we came?"

"We go right. We'll make our way through the trees — no noise — and we should see train tracks." She certainly hoped so. Otherwise, they may as well sit down and wait for morning.

They continued through the forest, arms out in front to avoid bashing their faces against tree trunks, placing their feet down as silently as possible. The only light was cast by patches of sky overhead. In the lead, Ashley strained to locate any sign of the switchyard.

After what seemed like hours of walking, they stumbled from the woods into an open area.

Jane looked up. "The freaking clouds are hiding the moon. It's too dark to see anything clearly. How are we supposed to find Lennon and Hank?" Her foot bumped against a rail track, and she flailed her arms to regain her balance. "Well, crap."

"Give me a minute. And, keep it down." Ashley stood motionless, hearing nothing but her friends breathing. "Okay, the tree line is to our left. We follow it."

Ashley headed off, with Jane and Crystal trailing. It kind of bugged her how she always knew where Lennon was. Even at school, with all the chatter and motion in the halls, she could find him as easily as though he had a laser shining out of the top of his head. What was that all about?

In the silence of this creepy, dead place, she sensed his position exactly.

She whispered his name.

"Here," came the muffled response.

Lennon lay face down on the ground. Hank crouched nearby, emitting soft mewling sounds of distress.

"What happened to you?" Ashley tugged on his arm and rolled him over onto his back.

"Hank fell on me. I'm fine."

"Then get up. And, don't stand near Hank."

Crystal and Jane snickered, moving closer to Hank. They patted his furry arms and hugged him as though it had been days since they last saw him, not hours.

Lennon seemed anxious to explain. "I heard a noise a couple hundred yards inside the bush. Hank got scared and climbed a tree, and the branch gave out under his weight and he fell on me."

"Guess you shouldn't stand underneath Hank when he's perching on a tree branch. Now, has the boxcar been loaded yet? And where is it, by the way?"

"They finished loading about an hour ago. So, I guess that cracking sound I heard was you guys."

Ashley eyes strained to see through the blackness. "Not us. I heard it, too. Do you sense anything else out there?" This was a totally creepy place, creepier than an empty, ancient switchyard had any reason to be.

"Nothing close enough for me to make out. The boxcar is over there about a hundred yards straight on. They might throw in a few more supplies in the morning, but they usually head out about 6 a.m. That's only four hours from now."

Ashley shifted from foot to foot, feeling more uneasy by the second. She turned in a circle and stared into the woods, but nothing moved or made a sound.

"Wait," Jane said, leaving Hank with Crystal and approaching Lennon and Ashley. "Will they lock us in? That would turn this whole trip into a shit festival if we can't get out before the train reaches the camp."

Lennon scanned the woods behind them, seemingly as edgy as Ashley. "They don't lock anything. The boxcar is so rickety, the doors don't even slide smoothly or meet in the middle. There's a security guard who's supposed to keep watch on the boxcar but he takes off for a few hours after loading. He should be back soon, so we better get inside."

Suddenly, his eyes grew wide and locked at something over Ashley's right shoulder.

CHAPTER 14

A HOLLOW-FACED SPECTRE STOOD DIRECTLY behind Ashley, leaning into her, its essence a cloud of sorrow and longing. If it was alive, it would be pressed against her body. Ashley whipped her head from side to side, as though she detected a presence nearby. Her blonde ponytail rippled through the ghost's face, distorting the green outlines. When the shape re-formed, the ghost gazed mournfully at Ashley, its dead eyes like twin pools of black sludge.

Lennon grabbed Ashley by the sleeve of her coat and shoved her away from the ghost.

"Hey!" She knocked his hand aside. "What's with you?"

"Um, sorry. I thought Hank was going to step on you."

"Get real. He's nowhere near me. And, I can look after myself."

The ghost's form wavered and it made a move to follow Ashley. Not knowing what else to do, Lennon gave it a hard stare and willed the spectre to back off. He shivered as an iciness swept his body. But, it worked. The spectre's feet were rooted to the earth. Twisting and straining, it directed its empty eyes at Lennon and blinked out. It was there one second, and gone the next.

His chest heaving with relief, and shivering with cold, Lennon motioned behind him. "Over here. We better get settled before the guard comes back." Holy hell, what would happen if the spectre had been able to follow them? Would they have a ghost on board the rail car the whole trip?

"Well, put your super hearing to use and listen for the guard." Ashley had attached a bulging black garbage bag to her backpack. She dumped it on the ground and tore open the top. A jumble of clothes fell onto the gravel.

She picked up a handful and thrust it into Lennon's arms. "Here. I found these in my garage when I was looking for my dad's back holster for my dagger. I think the jacket should fit. There's a toque and scarf and some gloves. I didn't have time to wash them, but they aren't too bad."

Lennon didn't move. "Is this okay with your dad?" The black bomber jacket was down-filled and had a hood.

"He moved to Edmonton two years ago. He's bought new stuff. My mom would have thrown all this out if she knew it was still in the garage."

Lennon shrugged out of his leather jacket and shoved it into his backpack. By the time he got the new gear on, Ashley and the other girls were stuffing Hank into a brown, quilted jacket almost the same colour as his fur. Crystal and Jane giggled madly as they zipped him up and added a hat with flaps like crazy trappers wore in movies.

Lennon eyed the Sasquatch and wished he had a phone so he could take a picture, to have later when Hank was back with his family. "He's got fur. I don't think he needs a coat. Or hat."

"How do you know he isn't cold?" Ashley crumpled up the plastic bag and pushed it into her backpack. "He doesn't talk. Maybe his kind hibernate in winter and he's not used to cold weather."

Hank looked down at himself and slapped his chest. "Mulleerf!"

"He talks. Just in a foreign language," Lennon mumbled.

Ashley watched Hank beat his chest and hop from foot to foot. The flaps of the red and black checked hat swung up and down. "He acts like a gorilla. Are you sure ...?"

"I'm sure. The guard is coming back. Let's move."

He led the girls and Hank over a minefield of

63

tracks that circled around and criss-crossed the switchyard. A solitary engine faced into the darkness of the forest. Behind it waited a wooden boxcar that, even in the night gloom, looked battered and neglected.

The wide, double doors lay invitingly open, but were at least five feet above ground level. Lennon scooped up Jane and tossed her inside, then did the same for Crystal, throwing their gear after them. He was kind of afraid to touch Ashley who, he knew from past experience, wouldn't hesitate to kick him in the groin or grind an elbow into his ribs.

Hank picked up Ashley between his massive hands. She clung to her backpack as the Sasquatch threw her into the boxcar after her friends. Lennon cringed when he heard her cursing out the "big, stupid monkey." Better Hank than him.

CHAPTER 15

ASHLEY CRAWLED ON HER HANDS and knees, checking out the space. Boxes of food and bottled water covered half of the boxcar which was the length of two house trailers. She crouched with her friends on the floor on the opposite side of the supplies and hoped they wouldn't be spotted by the railway workers if more staples were loaded. Chances weren't great they'd escape discovery, especially with a snuffling, grunting animal to hide. Hank was epic smelly, too.

A blur of motion whirled around her as Lennon re-arranged the piles of goods. She had never seen him move so fast. Not even when they were fighting the outlaw bikers who had infected him and were trying to eliminate him because he wasn't "getting the job done", meaning he hadn't made the requisite three kills to show his loyalty and earn his place in their gang of *ascended* beings.

In less than a minute, Lennon created an empty space behind the piles. Once the four of them and their gear — plus Hank — hunkered down with their knees up around their ears, they hadn't a spare centimetre of floor to stretch out in.

"We need to keep really still and quiet," Lennon whispered.

No sooner had the words left his mouth than a dark form appeared at the opening. Or, at least the head and torso of a form. A powerful beam from the guard's LED flashlight swept the interior of the boxcar.

Ashley heard the man sniff, then sniff again more deeply. Fearing he smelled Hank, Ashley squinched her eyes tightly shut, expecting to be discovered any second.

"Damn salami," the man muttered. The light receded and she heard him sliding the doors together. He slammed them several times before he was satisfied they were secure. His footfalls crunched across the gravel and finally faded away.

Lennon peered through a gap in the wooden slats. He drew back, uttering something that sounded like, "Whoa, he walked right through them."

"What did you say? Walked through what?" Ashley was horrified to find she was clutching Lennon's arm like a scared little girl. She slid as far away from him as she could, which was like three centimetres at the most.

"Uh, nothing. Never mind." Lennon pressed against the rickety boards, like he was trying to get away from her, too.

"Well, where is he?" Ashley used her elbow to gain more distance between them. This forced her against Jane who had her arms around Hank. Crystal was doing the same on Hank's other side.

"He's gone into the woods, probably to, you know. He'll stick around until the train leaves." Lennon shifted next to her and Ashley figured she was going to go nuclear if she had to stay here another minute, let alone hours. Now was no time to give in to the claustrophobia she never mentioned to anyone. Her legs were cramped with her pack lodged between her body and a stack of wooden food crates. Which, now she had time to notice, smelled of fresh oranges. Her mouth watered. She loved oranges.

"I could use a pee, too." Crystal's voice sounded muffled, her head pressed against Hank's fur. Couldn't smell very nice in there, for crap's sake.

Ashley snapped at her. "I said to go in the woods before we reached the switchyard. You'll just have to hold it."

"I did go in the woods!" Crystal whimpered.

"Well, nobody pees in here and keep your voices down." Lennon reached up and grabbed an armful of oranges from the crate above him. He threw one each to Jane and Crystal and two to Hank. He handed another two to Ashley, keeping one for himself. "I don't think they'll miss these off the top of the pile. Keep your peels and give them to Hank. He eats everything, and we don't want to leave evidence behind. We have to ride back on this train, and we don't want to alert the engineers or loggers that they had stowaways."

He leaned across Ashley and spoke to Crystal. "Which is why there is no peeing or anything else in here."

Crystal sighed. Her beads disappeared into Hank's fur as she laid her head on his shoulder. "Can I at least have some salami? The guard mentioned salami."

Ashley sat up straighter. She was starving and a couple of oranges weren't going to do the job. "Salami? Maybe it's Creminelli. That's Italian ..."

Lennon held his hand over his nose. "There'll be salami somewhere in these boxes, probably, but that's not what the guard smelled. Somebody stepped in bear crap and dragged it in here."

Ashley buried her nose in her handful of orange peels and tried not to gag.

CHAPTER 16

THE BLAST OF A TRAIN whistle jarred Lennon out of a light sleep. He looked through the slats and saw nothing but trees. Trees that went on forever. The train chugged onward and, since there were no junctions in the heart of the forest, Lennon figured the engineer simply wanted to relieve the monotony of the journey by sounding the whistle. Maybe, he warned a black bear or a moose too close to the track...

Lennon stiffened. Something scuttled across the roof of the boxcar. Turning up his hearing, he listened intently but the noise wasn't repeated. Perhaps, an overhanging tree branch brushed against the roof.

Without a watch or phone, he had no idea of the time, and the sky outside was obscured by the forest of towering Douglas firs lining the tracks.

Ashley's head rested on his shoulder, and he was sure she was going to give him the snake eye when she woke up. Still, he let her head rest, not minding the smell of her blonde hair inches from his nose. She breathed quietly which was more than he could say for the other three. He was used to Hank's loud snores but was surprised that both Jane and Crystal slept with their mouths open, emitting varying snuffles and snorts. Jane wore Hank's trapper hat. Only Lennon had woken at the train whistle and heard the faint sound from above their heads.

After the train departed Spirit Switchyard on the dot of 6 a.m. — according to know-it-all Ashley with the fancy phone — they had placed their packs on top of the food containers. This gave them more room to stretch, but their legs had cramped so badly, they had been forced to alternate standing and sitting.

Lennon's right leg was kinked, and he was losing feeling from the knee down. Still, he didn't want to disturb Ashley, telling himself he was just putting off the pain when she woke up and elbowed him in the ribs. He reached up and snagged another orange from the crate, carefully placing the peels into his pocket to give to Hank later.

He watched a King Kong-sized spider scurry across the ceiling. The spider didn't seem to realize it was winter.

He eyed the crate of oranges. Uh, maybe the spider hitched a ride from some tropical country where the spiders grew big and hairy. Like a tarantula.

Just as he considered using his super speed to swipe the spider to the ground and nudge it through one of the wider cracks in the boxcar wall, Hank stirred and opened his eyes. He lifted his head and sniffed the air. His nose twitched as he scrutinized his surroundings.

Did he see the giant spider? Nope. The sniffing increased in speed and intensity. Lennon shook Ashley. "Wake up. I think our stop is coming up."

Ashley leaped to her feet and said to Jane and Crystal. "Up and at 'em, girlfriends. Time to go."

Lennon kept his attention off the ceiling. Ashley wouldn't scream, but Crystal would for sure. Maybe Jane, too. He couldn't take a chance on the engineer and whoever else was in the engine car hearing them.

"What, what?" Crystal blinked and ran her tongue over her lips. "Are we there yet? I really have to pee, and I'm serious."

Ashley prodded Jane with her foot. "Up, sleeping beauty. We're out of here. Grab your gear."

Lennon and Hank each yanked on a door. In less than a minute, they created a gap wide enough for humans and Hank to exit. They sat on the floor with their legs dangling over the edge.

"Here's the plan," Lennon told the girls. "At the next bend in the tracks, when the engine is out of sight but before this boxcar follows, I'll give the word and we'll throw our packs into the trees. Then, when I call 'go', we jump off. We have to clear the tracks or the rear wheels will run over us. Once you land, stay down until the train is out of sight. Got it?"

Three heads nodded and scared eyes focussed on Lennon's lips as though fearful of missing a crucial word. Even Ashley didn't argue with him or try and change the plan to something she thought would be better. Lennon touched Hank's arm reassuringly, hoping his friend would jump at the same time.

At the next bend, Lennon whispered, "Toss." Four packs sailed off the boxcar. He had to be careful not to use his super strength, afraid his pack would smash against a tree trunk or fly so deeply into the forest, that he would waste precious time recovering it.

Before the boxcar followed the engine around the bend, and the engineer saw them leap out if he happened to look in his mirror, Lennon whispered, "Go. Go!"

CHAPTER 17

LENNON LEAPED HAND-IN-HAND WITH HANK and realized that Crystal would not land clear of the wheels. With his free arm, he reached back and snatched her out of the air. The three hit the ground and rolled to a stop. Or, two of them stopped.

Hank's sturdy body kept on tumbling until he disappeared into the trees, the hem of the brown coat flipping up around his waist. Lennon shoved Crystal's head to the ground and lay as still as possible until the back of the boxcar rumbled around the bend. He pushed himself up, searching for Jane and Ashley. Relief flooded him when he saw them getting to their feet close by. He ran back along the track to retrieve the four backpacks. Hank ambled out of the forest and dropped onto the crunchy-cold ground beside Jane and Ashley.

"What time is it?" Lennon asked.

"It's pee time," Crystal whooped. She disappeared behind the closest tree.

Jane and Ashley followed her while Lennon and Hank took a few steps in the other direction. "Don't go far," Lennon warned.

In three minutes they re-assembled, no one speaking as they pulled out bottled water and snacks. Lennon handed Hank the rest of the carrots and the orange peels from his pocket.

Ashley scrunched up an energy bar wrapper and looked at her phone. "It's 10:23 a.m. We've been travelling for over four hours. I hope Hank knows his way from here because I sure don't want to wander around in the forest. Probably no human has stepped on this ground in, like, ever." She glared up at the sky where the weak, winter sun cast no warmth on the earth below. The temperature would be lower in the forest. "It might snow."

She was exaggerating, but Lennon thought it unwise to comment so he concentrated on Hank's behaviour. Lennon was sure his friend had tried to tell him he wanted to get off the train. The sniffing and rapid breathing could have been an indication that he sensed his home nearby, right? But, now, he was acting like a playful puppy, running away from Crystal and Jane, then coming back and pretending to pounce on them. They couldn't just hop back on the train on its return run and leave Hank by himself at the edge of the track.

Lennon felt Ashley's eyes boring into the side of his head. He better get them moving. "Hey, Hank," he called. "Come on, buddy. Show us where to find your family."

Hank stood up and faced the trees. He stretched his neck up and inhaled. "Zamph. Kikim."

"What'd he say?" Ashley asked Lennon.

He shrugged. "Don't have a clue. I told you he doesn't speak English."

"Well, what time does the train come back this way?"

"I don't know that either. It might take another four or five hours for it to reach the logging camp, then unload and not reach us for six to seven hours after that. It has to be back at Spirit Junction so they can load up again."

Ashley's blue eyes narrowed into slits, not a good sign. "Too bad you didn't find out what time the train gets back to Spirit Switchyard after its run. We could've calculated how long until it reaches this spot again. I believe you mentioned that the train doesn't run on Sundays, so we have to catch it back tonight. If we miss it, we'll be stuck freezing our asses off until Monday. By then, there will be land and air searches and, hello, we're all in deep trouble. Including you. Unless we're all dead from exposure."

Lennon tried to reassure her. "You can relax. We won't be here all night." Oops, he just thought of a small hitch. Since tomorrow was Sunday, the train wouldn't load tonight. What if the crew took their time on the return trip today or, worse, didn't bother to return until sometime tomorrow? He wouldn't mention that possibility to the girls right now.

Ashley opened her mouth to argue, no surprise, and Jane stepped between them. "Uh, Ash. You were the one who insisted we tag along to make sure Hank gets back to his family. We didn't exactly plan this out, so it's not Lennon's fault."

"He did try and talk us out of coming with him," Crystal added. "I think we need to see this through. Things will work out for us. They usually do."

"Fine." Ashley bent to pick up her pack. "I'm out-voted by a rationalist and an optimist."

She glared at Lennon but, before she could label him, and he was sure it wouldn't be flattering, Jane waved her phone. "I have one bar. What's the name of the logging company? Maybe we can learn the location of their camp. How far away it is, I mean, so we have a better idea when the train might come back this way."

"Dennison Jackson," Crystal responded. "They have permission to take down some of the old growth trees and my parents are part of an activist group trying to get their license revoked. I'm not sure where the camp is, but it's likely near the logging site."

"Well, let's just see," Jane mumbled, thumbs flying across the screen. "Okay, we're here, and the camp is

..." She looked up, then over at the trees, then across the tracks. "Um ..."

Crystal yelled, "Hey, Hank, come back here. Wait for us!"

Hank's brown backside disappeared into the dense forest. Lennon rushed ahead of the girls to keep him in sight. He experienced a brief blip of resistance, like he was pressing against a balloon, then it was gone, and he used his super speed to catch up and put a restraining hand on Hank's arm.

Hank stopped and they waited for the girls. Ashley reached them first, her chest heaving. "Did you feel that? When we entered the forest? Like we were touching something but it gave way?"

Before Lennon could answer, Crystal and Jane rushed up, both gasping for air. Crystal rested her forehead against the trunk of a towering Douglas fir. "I had a strange feeling back there. Kind of like the trees didn't want me to pass. Now I need to go again, if you catch my drift. So, you can all wait for me or leave. But, I'm going to pee." She disappeared behind a fir.

Jane frowned and wiped her forehead with her sleeve. "I think it was a giant web we ran through. I don't want to run into the spider that can spin a web that strong. Come on, Crystal, hurry up."

Lennon caught Ashley rolling her eyes but looked away before those eyes settled on him. What was her problem, now? Still clutching Hank's furry arm, he waited until Crystal re-appeared and said, "We better keep moving."

Every so often, Hank sped out of sight and Lennon had to go after him and hold him steady until the girls caught up. The trunks of the Douglas firs were so enormous, it was easy to lose sight of one or more members of the party. Crystal, especially, had a talent for vanishing, but Lennon always found her no more than a tree or two away.

At one point, he stopped and gathered everyone together. "Listen, it's so dark in here, it'll be easy to lose someone. So, if one of you doesn't see the rest of us, just stop and yell, 'hold'. I'll come and find you. Agreed?"

"We all agree." Ashley spoke for her friends. "Jane, where's the logging site or camp from here."

Jane shook her phone. "Got no bars in this cursed forest. Just the black screen of no-internet. I can't tell the time either."

They craned their necks to see slivers of visible sky beyond the tips of the firs.

"These trees must be 50 feet high," Ashley guessed.

"More like 200 to 300 feet," Crystal corrected her. "Too bad one of us isn't wearing an old-timey watch."

"It must be noon at least." Ashley picked up her backpack. "Guess we better keep going. Does anyone have an idea which way the tracks are? We could be going in circles."

"Hank?" Lennon looked around.

Hank had slipped away while Lennon was distracted, listening to the waste-of-time jibber-jabber. "Stay here. I'll be right back."

In a flash, he was gone.

CHAPTER 18

THE GIRLS PLOPPED DOWN ON the floor of the forest and rummaged in their packs for food and water. Ashley heard Lennon off in the distance calling Hank's name but, within a few minutes, the forest was silent except for raucous bird calls high in the branches.

She took off her glove and patted the earth. "Is it my imagination, or is it a lot warmer in here than out in the open. The ground isn't frozen. It's damp, like in the summer."

They stood up before their jeans soaked up more moisture.

"That's strange," Crystal said. She removed her knitted hat and gloves, shoving them into the outside flap of her pocket. "I thought running was making me sweat, but the temperature is definitely higher here. It should be a lot cooler."

Jane pointed to a small clearing nearby where the ground was dappled with sunlight. "I'm no botanist, but shouldn't ferns be shrivelled up, waiting for spring."

"Those are sword ferns." Crystal walked into the clearing and squatted. "They shouldn't be so green and lush, and see this clump of little yellow flowers? Skunk cabbage. They bloom in spring, not in January."

"I didn't want to mention it, but I thought I smelled a skunk." Ashley followed Crystal to the clearing.

"Um, that's why it's called skunk cabbage." Crystal bent her head closer to the ground. "And, here's a couple of white fawn lilies, also a spring flower. Both these species usually grow in the coastal regions of the forest. Problem is, I think we're in the interior of the island. Or, should be."

Jane came up to stand behind her friends. "Climate change?"

"Probably, but this is pretty extreme."

Ashley pulled out her phone and held it over her head. She spun around, hoping to catch a bar. "Absolutely nothing. Can't even take pictures of these freaky plants to post on social media so the climate change deniers can try to explain it away."

"Duh, Ashley," Jane aimed her phone at the flowers. "Guess you've never been in an out-ofservice situation before. Photos can be taken. We just can't send them out."

"Really?" Ashley paused to watch Jane snap a dozen pictures of the unseasonal plants. "How did I not know that?"

"I wonder what time it is." Crystal rotated her shoulders and head in a circle, sending her braids flying. "How long did we run, do you think?"

"Twenty minutes?" Jane looked confused. "I hope Lennon didn't get lost."

Ashley slammed her useless phone into her pack. "We ran longer than twenty minutes. Maybe an hour? And, FYI, we're lost with or without Lennon. If he found Hank and his family, he might have a chance to survive with a herd of furry, warm animals who will feed him. We don't have a prayer."

"You're always such a pessimist." Crystal pointed behind them. "We should go back and wait where Lennon said to, so he can find us after he finds Hank and comes back for us."

"And, just where would that be?" Jane eyed the forest surrounding the tiny clearing. "These giant trees all look alike. Anybody count how many steps we took to get here?"

"I took twelve steps," Ashley said. She pointed. "From over there." She was positive, although she couldn't explain how.

She took twelve steps in the direction her instincts pulled her. Her friends followed. "See, here's my butt print where I sat on the ground. We'll wait here for a while." She may not be a smart phone expert, but she was good with directions. Usually. This forest was proving a challenge.

"How long? And, what do we do when we're done waiting?" Jane stripped off her parka and stuffed it away. She unzipped her vest and folded her arms. "We won't freeze, but we might starve to death."

"Let's face it," Crystal said. "We're lost and we're going to die. Nobody knows we hitched a ride on the train into the interior ..."

"Shsst," Ashley snapped. "Listen."

After an interval, Crystal ventured, "I don't hear anything except the creepy birds."

"Yes, but underneath that, what do you hear?"

"There's nothing *underneath*, Ash. Just birds."

Jane held up her hand. "I get what you mean. The birds are making the only sounds, except for us."

"Exactly." Ashley was relieved someone else noticed. "A forest is never totally silent. The branches creak and rub together. There should be wind gusts, and small animals stepping on twigs, and larger ones crashing through the brush."

"In fact," a deeper voice commented. "We're hearing only one type of bird."

CHAPTER 19

"SORRY," LENNON SAID, WHEN THE three girls ceased squealing at his sudden re-appearance. Well, two of them squealed. Ashley gave him a fiery-eyed glare that made him move farther away.

But, all she said was, "You're right. There's more than one bird, but the same call."

Jane slapped Lennon on the back, in welcome he hoped. "Now that I think about it, in a forest you hear dozens of different birds. Here there's only a croaky thing. Can't even call it a song. More like a bullfrog except it's coming from the trees."

Relieved at Lennon's return, Crystal gave him a hug. Holding on to him for a minute, she said, "Some frogs mate at this time of year, so maybe that's what it is, although the sound is kind of loud for frogs."

"Can we stop talking about frogs?" Ashley pointed up at the high branches. "That noise is from a raven. Actually, a bunch of ravens. They're calling to each other, and there are either a lot of them, or they've been following us since we ran into the forest after Hank." She looked at Lennon. "Guess you didn't find him."

Lennon extricated himself from Crystal. "I followed his footprints for a while, but he must have climbed up and is travelling from tree to tree. He wouldn't come when I called. I guess we won't see him again." He shook off the grief that enveloped him. Hank was never going to stay with him for good. He knew that from the moment he saw Hank and took him home.

Lennon returned his attention to Ashley. She stood completely still and, at the next raven call, whipped her head around and said softly, "There to my right, about 25 feet up. See that splotch of white? There's another one a few branches higher. They may sound like ravens, but they're white instead of black. Don't make a sound. See if you can find more."

Crystal started to sit down, then remembering the damp, spongy ground, bobbed up again. "Now that I'm looking for white birds, I can make out a couple up there."

While the girls squinted at the nearby trees, Lennon focussed his enhanced vision far into the forest. Even for him, the ravens were difficult to make out at first because they perched on the branches like stuffed owls, without movement. Their beaks were as white as their feathers and, once he knew what to look for, they stood out as clearly as mounds of snow against a wooden fence.

"I count at least 20," he finally said. Aware of the sweat running down his neck and spine, he removed the winter wear Ashley had given him and crammed it all into his backpack. "By the racket, I'm guessing there are more. They seem to be communicating with each other."

"White ravens are rare," Crystal said. "It's odd to find so many in one spot."

"Everything about this place is odd." Jane blotted her forehead with the hem of her shirt. "I'd really like to leave now and catch a train back to civilization where my phone works. I'd love to do a web search on white ravens. Not ever."

Lennon stared at the silhouette of a raven perched motionless on a branch a hundred feet up. "These guys have blue eyes, not red, so does that mean they aren't true albinos?"

"Gee-zuz." Ashley rolled her eyes. "There's a small colony of white ravens with blue eyes living near Qualicum Beach north of Nanaimo. Blue eyes mean they're the product of a genetic defect that dilutes their colour, not albinos that have red eyes. I never heard of them living this far inland, though.

And, they only travel in flocks before mating and staking out their own territory."

"So, it's not common to see this many genetically-mutated ravens in a flock in this area? Does that about sum it up?" Jane looked at Ashley like she was some kind of freak. "How do you know all that?"

"I guess you weren't paying attention in biology class last year when we learned the differences between crows and ravens, and the white colony on the island was discussed." Ashley managed to look superior as she gave her lips another layer of shiny gloss.

Lennon said, "I don't think we're seeing that colony from Qualicum Beach. Everything about this section of the forest is ... different."

Ashley looked above Lennon's head, her hand moving to grip the hilt of the blade lying flat against her back. When he turned to see what had captured her attention, he made eye contact with a raven that had silently hopped from somewhere high in the trees to a branch not two metres from the teens. A single splash of black the size of a loonie lay over its breast.

The bird cocked its head and stared him down. Lennon averted his eyes and noted that Ashley had lowered her hand to her side.

She swept aside the damp strands of hair plastered against her forehead. "Let's recap, shall we? We can't remember how long or far we ran. We don't know what time it is. The temperature in this eerie place is like a tropical rainforest. There are no sounds except the calls from a flock of white ravens that shouldn't be here at all. Oh, and we have no idea where we are or how to get back to where we started. Have I missed anything?"

CHAPTER 20

LENNON CLEARED HIS THROAT. WHEN everyone turned to look at him, he took a deep breath and announced, "Someone placed a ward on this part of the forest."

Jane's face formed the expression he hadn't seen for a few months, since the girls thought he was a vampire and tried to kill him every time they caught sight of him.

Her fair skin flushed. "Awarded? Awarded what? The designation of creepiest place on the island, maybe on earth?"

"Warded, not awarded!" he repeated and stepped back from her. Jane was small but fast, and the tips of her spiked red hair seemed to vibrate with rage. "Like in magically protected."

Jane was stunned into silence. Crystal's fingers

went to her mouth as she bit down on her cuticles. She looked at her grubby fingers and spat on the ground.

Ashley's expression turned stony. "Okay, a bunch of questions. How do you know there's a ward, who raised it; and why were we able to walk through it? Although I'm guessing we all felt that resistance when we first ran into the forest after Hank." Ashley bit off each word and stepped closer to Lennon, shoving Jane out of the way.

Lennon thought it interesting she didn't have a problem with the existence of wards or magic. "The answer to all your questions is, I haven't a clue. I'm not even sure 'ward' is the right word. But something is hiding this place from the rest of the world."

Crystal cleaned her fingers with a tiny bottle of hand sanitizer that smelled like watermelon. "Witches use wards. I'm seriously weirded out."

Ashley flapped her hand at Crystal in dismissal. "Knock it off. We've been in worse situations. This shouldn't be a problem. No armed killers or crazy-ass ninjas in here. We assume Hank has been reunited with his family, and we'll eventually find our way out. Simple."

"Well," Lennon hated to burst her bubble, especially because she could turn mean in a flash, but ...

"Spitting it out would be good, Lennon," Ashley warned.

"Okay! I found the logging camp. They were

unloading food supplies from a truck. Which means the train tracks are some distance from the camp, and the train has ... um ..."

"Left the station," Crystal finished for him. "This forest is cursed, and we couldn't hear the train if it passed 100 metres away."

Ashley stared down two white ravens sitting on the lowest branch of a nearby tree. Her arm reached over her shoulder again to touch the hilt of her dagger. "Pretty sure we're a lot farther from the tracks than that."

The black-spotted raven hopped from one foot to the other, then turned to face the pure white bird sharing its branch. They made their low croaking noise, and it seemed to Lennon that they were laughing. He didn't feel threatened but slid his hand into his pack to reassure himself that he could get at the curved knife he had taken several months ago from the body of an infected biker who chased him across the Trans-Canada Highway. It wasn't Lennon's fault the biker got hit by a transport.

"Can you find the camp again?" Ashley's hand closed over her dagger's hilt but she didn't draw it from its sheath. "How close did you get to it?"

"Close. I counted eleven loggers. They should have been able to see me, but they didn't. Their voices were muted, but I could make out their words."

Ashley grunted in frustration. "I guess we'll have

to leave this magical place and ask the loggers to help us get back home."

"Yeah, that should be our last option."

"It's our only option!" Ashley screamed. "You said yourself the train is gone and there won't be another one until Monday. I'm guessing this is still Saturday, although who knows — it could be Wednesday, July 1st in the year 2042!"

Jane piped up, "If my phone worked, I could check that date for you."

Ashley whirled on her friend. "You think this is funny? I admit it was my stupid idea to come here in the first place but, if we didn't, Lennon would be wandering lost in here by himself. At least we're together." She looked confused at her own words, as though wondering why they should care about him.

She turned her fury on Lennon. "Explain why we can't go to the loggers for help. And, just say it, for crying out loud."

"Sure," he conceded. "Loggers usually carry rifles or shotguns in case they're attacked by bears or cougars. I saw a couple of rifles leaning up against a hut. But, they also had handguns in holsters strapped to their belts. What do you think they need those for?"

As Ashley got set to argue with him, Lennon followed her directive and spat the rest out before she could harangue him further. "They were talking about 'taking care' of some 'freaks and weirdos' in the forest, making sure they didn't try and stop them from logging in this area, where I gather they don't have a license."

"Do they mean us?" Crystal chimed in. "How would they even know about us? We just got here."

Jane snickered. "Unless it really is 2042." She ignored Ashley's death glare.

"They weren't talking about us," Lennon said. "I don't think we're alone in here."

CHAPTER 21

ASHLEY POSITIONED HER BACKPACK EVENLY across her shoulders, making sure she could reach her dagger. "We need to see the logging camp."

"I left some markers so we wouldn't get turned around." Lennon had broken off small fronds from the ferns that carpeted the forest floor, using clumps of wet earth to glue the fronds to tree trunks. He moved confidently through the forest, winding around the colossal trunks. The white ravens croaked to each other and followed.

He may have been trying to moderate his pace, but Ashley was soon drenched in sweat from running along behind him. She looked back every few seconds to make sure her friends were still in sight. Her tee shirt was sopping wet, and she pushed the sleeves up to her elbows. "I can almost hear myself sweat. I'm going to break out in fungus any time now."

Crystal giggled. "Hopefully, we'll grow edible mushrooms on our bodies."

"I don't believe you've said anything grosser in all the years I've known you," Jane offered, shoving Crystal in the shoulder from her place at the back of the line. "Let's speed this up. I think those white birds are making fun of us."

After an hour's walk — or it could have been five hours or ten minutes, since the passage of time seemed altered in the forest — Lennon stopped abruptly. "Over there."

He pointed to the right, and Ashley turned to face a shifting haze visible between the trees only metres away. At first, she thought it was fog but, instead of vapour, the air rippled as though what lay beyond was under water.

Lennon strode toward the heaving curtain, and Ashley motioned for her friends to hang back. "Stay here. I'll check it out with Lennon, then when I'm sure it's safe, I'll signal you."

Jane and Crystal leaned against a massive trunk and Crystal rubbed her shoulder blades against the rough bark. "This humidity is making me itchy all over. Which reminds me, how come we haven't been seen any mosquitoes or other bugs? It's warm enough."

Jane replied, "Because there's nothing but creepy, white birds and us in here. I wonder what they eat."

Their voices faded, and Ashley ran to catch up to Lennon. He stopped in front of the hazy ward — if that's what it was — and pointed. "See that?"

She was sure she could reach out and thrust her arm right through the surging curtain. She didn't chance it, not knowing how magic worked. Maybe touching it would break the spell. And, she didn't want that to happen. Or, maybe ... She remembered the resistance they felt as they entered the forest. That was the ward and their entrance hadn't broken it.

On the other side lay a large encampment created by the felling of a dozen primordial giants. The trunks had been chain-sawed into manageable pieces and hauled away, leaving an open area covered with stumps, each large enough to hold a one-man tent. Excavating equipment dotted the areas between the stumps. Tarps suspended from poles sheltered dozens of chainsaws. Ashley noticed the rifles leaning against the rough-hewn log walls of several outhouses.

A road led into the camp and circled back on itself, wide enough to accommodate a flatbed truck's coming and goings. The flatbed was empty, and the cab door didn't display a company name.

In the camp, it was winter. Eleven men — if Lennon counted right — were bundled in heavy jackets and boots, most wearing toques. Their faces were unshaven, some with beards. Without exception, holstered handguns hung from their belts.

From one of the tents, a man passed out cans and

bottles to waiting hands. One of the loggers clinked his can against the bottle of a buddy. By the shape of the bottle, it was whiskey or another liquor. "Hope we have enough to last until Monday," he said. "This no-Sunday delivery is getting old."

"Maybe you need to pace yourself," suggested his friend, swigging back his whiskey, "or switch to this good stuff. A little goes a long way."

Ashley glanced at Lennon and opened her mouth to ask why he had told them that sounds from the other side were muffled. There was nothing muted about the conversation between the two loggers. Lennon held up a hand and pointed across the clearing beyond the tents and outbuildings where living, massive firs loomed over the camp, waiting their turn to fall to the loggers' chainsaws.

At first, Ashley couldn`t see anything between the colossal trunks, but then ... "Are those people? With cloaks and hoods?" Crap, what new hell was about to hit them now? Was it her imagination, or did the rippling air that separated them from the logging camp appear thinner than a few minutes ago, the murkiness dissipating?

"Must be the freaks and weirdos the loggers were talking about."

Dark figures darted among the shadows in the forest. Ashley couldn't tell how many there were.

She pulled on Lennon's arm. "I hope they have some weapons hidden inside their robes, or it's going to be an uneven fight, and I'm not getting in the middle of it. We should head back."

The loggers' heads jerked up, but they didn't turn to look behind them at the four robed figures who had left the forest and crept across the clearing towards the tents. The loggers stared directly at Lennon and Ashley.

Definitely, the haze was waning. Fast. "Uh oh. I think they can see and hear us. I thought you said this place was protected by some kind of magic." Ashley stood perfectly still, hoping she was wrong. Maybe the loggers spied the white ravens. The rippling curtain had mostly disappeared, and she could see the loggers as clearly as she could hear them. Nope, not good.

The two loggers called to their friends, then beer-can guy shouted at Ashley and Lennon. "You in there. Come out now! This is private property and you have no business here." His hand reached for his gun.

Lennon jumped behind a trunk, pulling Ashley with him.

"The ward is broken."

CHAPTER 22

ASHLEY DROPPED TO HER KNEES and peered around the enormous trunk at the scene unfolding like a movie. The loggers spread out and halted at the edge of the tree line, peering into the gloom, waving their guns from side to side, searching. They remained unaware of the invading, cloak-clad figures behind them.

While the white ravens called out warnings, a second band of four figures raced silently onto the scene from the direction of the dirt road, leaping lightly from stump to stump, advancing on the cloaked figures. This group reminded Ashley of Ninja Boy who had fought with Grey Jacket in the park last night — dressed entirely in black with their heads and faces wrapped except for their eyes. It didn't look to Ashley like the ninjas were here to back up the cloaked figures. She was suddenly sure the ninjas and cloaks were about to do battle, with the loggers caught in the middle. Where did that leave Ashley and her friends?

Once on clear ground, the ninjas took combative stances as they advanced in a V-formation, one man in front, one man slightly behind on either side. The fourth fighter stayed back and monitored the perimeter.

Ashley jumped a foot when she felt a touch on her shoulder. She whirled and looked up into the horrified faces of her friends. Lennon shifted to make room for Jane and Crystal to squat beside them.

The ninjas advanced on the hooded figures who threw their cloaks over their shoulders to reveal black pants and shirts before assuming similar fighting postures as the ninjas. Ashley was so entranced by the spectacle of two fighting factions moving soundlessly behind the loggers, she forgot to be afraid of the armed loggers.

Four cloaks clashed with four ninjas directly behind the loggers who finally noticed the near-silent battle raging at their backs and turned away from the forest to watch, guns ready but unable to fix on the targets moving almost too fast to see. Flesh slammed against flesh as kicks and thrusts landed in a flurry of movements.

Lennon got to his feet behind Ashley. She looked up at him to ask what the hell was happening but realized from his rounded eyes and clenched jaw that he had no more clue than she did.

The loggers lost focus and milled around in disarray, shouting to one another and to the combatants. Many held their guns in firing position, but no shots had been fired so far. Maybe, since no one was beating on them, the loggers thought it prudent to wait until one group defeated the other before taking on the survivors.

Lennon finally shook off his fascination with the battle and said to Ashley, "This is a good time to get as far away from here as we can. Hold hands and follow me. Be as quiet as possible."

Grabbing Ashley's hand, he set off through the maze of primal giants. Ashley made sure Jane took the rear before clutching Crystal's hand. Lennon maintained a normal running pace, but in minutes Ashley struggled to keep up.

They stopped to rest and the girls sank to the ground, not caring that the damp earth soaked their jeans to the skin.

Ashley noticed something odd. "Hear that? No ravens."

"Yeah, cool ... say, Ash ..." Crystal gasped for air. "Didn't those guys with their heads wrapped ... in black cloth ..." Her words tumbled out in waves. "... remind you of Ninja Boy?"

"Who's Ninja Boy?" Lennon asked. He had stationed himself at a neighbouring trunk, scanning the forest for signs of danger.

"Remember, we started telling you what happened on the way to your place from the dentist yesterday. We didn't get a chance to explain, what with you being so out of it, and Hank surprising us." Jane gulped the last third of a water bottle and thrust the empty into her pack. "Well, that's me officially out of water."

"I'm out, too," Ashley said. "My tongue is sticking to my teeth."

Jane grunted in agreement. "Shouldn't there be a lake or pond in here?"

"Yum. Pond water. We'll need a whole new set of vaccines for that," Crystal said, wringing out the hem of her shirt. "Yeewww. Do you think we'll be forced to drink our own body fluids? Like recycling?"

"To summarize," Ashley said to Lennon, ignoring her friends. "I haven't a clue who the cloaked people are, but the others wrapped in black from head to toe are after you. Hard as that is to believe."

"Oh, yeah, I figured that," Lennon said. "I told you I've been followed for the past couple of months, since I got the vaccine."

"Why didn't you tell us sooner?" Ashley tried to keep her voice down, but her words ended in a girly shriek.

Lennon avoided her eyes. "A bunch of people are coming, a couple hundred metres away. By the noise I hear, it's the loggers." His face hardened. "They have guns. We have to run."

"Just a minute." Ashley pulled Jane and Crystal

in closer. "They won't show us mercy, so we don't go down without a fight. Remember. We're warriors. If we're cornered, crouch behind a tree, pull out your weapons, and wait for them to move into sight. Jump out, aim for their gun hand first, and keep swinging."

She squeezed her friends in a quick hug, then turned to Lennon. "We're ready. You lead." Why were the loggers tracking four kids when they had eight interlopers right in front of them?

Lennon lifted his head and engaged his enhanced hearing, although by now the sounds of their pursuers were evident even to the girls — men's boots thudding against the damp ground and angry voices roaring curses at their quarry.

"We're going this way. Trust me." Instead of moving ahead of the loggers, Lennon chose a path at a right angle to their direction.

Was he trying to manoeuver around their flank and end up behind them? Ashley's fear urged her to run ahead of the loggers, but her instincts told her to trust him. "Okay, but you better not get us killed."

Suddenly, scores of white ravens swooped silently from the tree branches and dove over their heads, the black-spotted bird in the lead. Ashley was terrified the sharp beaks would stab her head. Her eyes ... Close by, Jane and Crystal squealed and shielded their heads with their arms.

"Never mind them," Lennon called. "They aren't going to hurt us. Follow me."

As the last raven glided over their heads, turning its wings to avoid the branches, the girls raced after Lennon.

The sounds of their passage through the forest concealed those of the loggers. Ashley hoped the reverse was true. But, if the loggers stood still, they would hear their targets.

A raven's cry echoed through the forest, deep and raspy, like a warning or a call to war. The other ravens answered the call. A multitude of harsh sounds resounded through the trees, the clamour of a hundred soldiers eager to roust an invading army.

A volley of gunshots sliced through the forest.

CHAPTER 23

"LET'S MOVE!" LENNON CALLED TO the girls, and they set off again, linking hands and darting around the trees. These trunks were less massive than the Douglas firs, and Lennon thought they might be Sitka spruce but he didn't take the time to ask Crystal who seemed to be the expert on forests.

The sound of the loggers' gunfire mingled with the ravens' calls, making it impossible for Lennon to guess who was winning even with his enhanced hearing. While this tumultuous fight raged behind them, Lennon thought about the silent battle taking place at the logging camp between two sets of unknown combatants. Which side was winning that fight? Did it even matter?

The ravens' cries halted abruptly. Was it over? Were the birds retreating? Or, dead? The booming gunfire continued for several seconds until it tapered off, leaving the forest silent.

"Oh god, oh god," Crystal whimpered. "Maybe the loggers are out of bullets. I can't run much farther."

"Probably re-loading," Jane huffed, from the back of the line. "I'll have to stop soon, too."

"I hope they didn't kill all the ravens," Ashley said. "The gunshots sound too far away for the loggers to be aiming at us. Maybe they're taking on the other guys."

"We're not stopping to find out." Lennon forged ahead, clutching Ashley's hand. As long as she kept hold of Crystal, and Crystal didn't let go of Jane, he meant to get them as far away from the loggers as possible. He gave up his plan to circle around the loggers and head away from the camp back to the train tracks. The warded forest had confused his sense of direction. Should he keep track of the loggers' position and head in the opposite direction, or not? With any luck, the loggers were disoriented, too, and wouldn't spread out to cut them off. Far ahead to his right, daylight shone through the trees, and he veered toward the source.

Slowly, the tall Sitka spruce and spongy forest floor gave way to smooth rocky ground and smaller species of pines. The temperature cooled slightly, but still more June than January. The brightness ahead appeared to be natural sunlight, and it drew him like a beacon of comfort. He marginally engaged his super speed in an effort to reach the light, towing the trio of girls behind him.

He burst through the trees and staggered to a halt, feeling the summer sun on his face. Ashley bumped up against his back, too breathless to do anything but look over his shoulder.

The forest surrounded acres of flat rock. The sun dazzled his eyes after the gloom of the woodland. Despite the welcoming warmth and light, he sensed peril nearby. He held out his arm to stop the girls from running past him into whatever was out there. "Wait here."

He stepped onto the rock and walked a few yards, stopping when his right foot hovered over empty space. Before he lost his balance, Lennon pulled his leg back onto solid rock. This was an optical illusion, fooling the eye into believing the rock covering this immense stone field was solid and unbroken when, in reality, he stood on the overhanging edge of a cliff. He looked down and released a pent up breath.

Ashley moved to stand beside him. He grabbed her arm as she puffed in his ear. "Sunlight at last. This clearing has to be 200 feet across. Good thing we didn't trip ..." She followed the line of his scrutiny. "Gee-zuz!" She motioned at her friends to join them.

Crystal and Jane tip-toed up beside Lennon and Ashley.

Jane glanced down and spewed out the cussing phrases and verbs she had been holding in all day.

The spikes of her hair stuck out in all directions, moisture running down the sides of her face.

"Ditto, what you said Jane," Crystal commented. "And, crappity-crap for good measure."

Far below, a lake lay at the bottom of the chasm, its waters a deep, opaque blue, impossible to know how deep. Could be a thousand feet, could be a hundred. Or just ten.

Lennon's heartbeats slowed and the pounding in his ears subsided, enabling him to hear the roaring sounds of fast-moving water resonating from his right side. Through a gap in the trees, a river transformed into a tumbling waterfall, cascading over the cliff, sending up sprays of sparkling foam as it emptied into the lake.

"Is this a volcanic crater?" Crystal asked. "I never heard of an ancient volcano anywhere on the Island. Maybe, we've discovered a new one and they'll name it after us."

"If we don't die in here first," Jane reminded them.

"Geez, have you guys ever paid attention in geography class?" Ashley threw her friends a disgusted look. "There are no volcanoes, active or extinct, on the Island. See that mountain peak? That's the Golden Hinde which means we're somewhere in the interior, maybe Strathcona Provincial Park, maybe in an alternate universe; who the hell knows?"

Lennon waited until she ran out of words. "We're

probably looking at a meteorite impact crater, maybe millions of years old. That would explain the rocky ground we ran through the last few miles."

"The crater could be billions of years old," Crystal offered, trying to wind stray strands of hair through her braids. "The earth is three billion years old, give or take a couple million. See, I know stuff, too."

Ashley turned her back to Crystal and glanced up at the sky. "I believe the sun is straight up at mid-day, no? My question is: what day? We got off the train about 10:30 Saturday morning. We've been running around in circles for more than a couple hours. Time is weird in here. I'd really like to know what day it is. Maybe it's Monday already and there's Amber alerts out on all of us. Except Lennon since no one will notice he's missing."

Pretending he didn't hear her last comment, Lennon dropped to his stomach and looked over the edge, hooking his fingers over rock worn smooth by millennia of exposure to the elements. What he saw didn't make him feel good about their chances for long-term survival. He engaged his enhanced sight and, there, at an outcropping of rock ledge near the bottom of the waterfall, he spied something else. It was a mere glimpse, but might explain why they stumbled on this place that seemed to be a death trap. He could get down there easy, but couldn't leave the others. He didn't believe they had time to go around the crater.

Jane crouched and searched through her pack. "I was hoping a bottle of water would miraculously appear in Oz or Narnia, or whatever magical kingdom we've landed in. But, nope."

Crystal had lost most of her skull beads, so the clacking was muted when she swung her braids. "If we go right, we could drink out of the river, but it might be too wide and fast-flowing to cross."

"Guess we go left, then," Jane answered, getting to her feet. "Maybe we'll find a stream we can drink from."

"Quiet." Lennon lifted his head and listened intently. "The loggers have found our trail. They're 20 minutes out, tops."

He shared a long look with Ashley and waited until he sensed her agreement.

Beckoning to her friends, Ashley drew them close and put her hands on their arms. "I don't know how those men are tracking us, but if we stay here, we're trapped. We have to do the unexpected."

"Don't like the sounds of that," Jane grumbled. "But, I guess this is literally the point of no return, so lead on, oh fearless one."

"As usual, we're gonna die," Crystal whimpered, but she squared her shoulders and threw back her unravelling dreadlocks. "So, which way are we going? And, please don't say back the way we came."

Ashley looked at Lennon and inclined her head.

Lennon's toes teetered on the edge of the overhang. "We're going down."

CHAPTER 24

"JUST TRUST US," ASHLEY PLEADED with her friends. "We have no choice. Even if those men are out of bullets, they can easily throw us off this cliff. The only chance we have is to get to the bottom before they reach us."

"We can't jump from here!" Crystal wailed. "The water might be only a few feet deep, even if we clear the rim of the lake. It's all rock and water!"

"We aren't jumping from here," Lennon told them. "There are a series of ledges below us, at least two I can make out, maybe more. The one directly under us is about ten feet down. The closer we can get to the water, the safer we are to jump. I'll lower myself down, then help you, one at a time. We keep that up until we run out of levels. We might not have to ..." He raised his head to listen. "They're 15 minutes away."

"Then, what?" Crystal asked, tears pooling in her dark eyes. "What do we do if we make it to the bottom? If we can get there alive, the loggers can, too."

"I have a plan," Lennon insisted. "We all go, or we all die here. Decide fast."

"Let's do it." Jane unzipped her backpack and wrapped her phone in her winter jacket. "I'm not leaving my stuff behind."

Lennon slid over the cliff, fingers pressed into the rock. He swung his body back and forth until he gathered the momentum to drop. Ashley handed down the four backpacks, then helped Jane hang over the edge. She waited for Lennon to acknowledge he had Jane by the waist before urging her friend to let go. No problem with Jane, but Crystal was a unicorn from a different herd.

Ashley heard the loggers bellowing in the distance. "Crystal, if you stay here, I have to stay with you. Then we both die for sure."

Whimpering, Crystal slid her body over the edge. Ashley lay flat on the overhang and held Crystal's hands. She didn't let go until she heard Lennon say, "Got her."

It was her turn. Without hesitation, Ashley turned her body and slithered over, feet first. Her fingernails scraped painfully as she gripped the smooth stone. She wondered fleetingly if she would ever experience the luxury of a manicure again before Lennon's arms encircled her thighs and pulled her in.

The ledge was roughly twelve by eight feet, the stone worn as smooth as the cliff above. Good thing it wasn't raining, or they'd slide right off. The thought made Ashley's stomach roll. To distract herself, she examined her friends' reactions as they plastered their backs against the wall of the cliff. Jane wore a stoic expression, clutching her pack, and Crystal moaned non-stop — so, basically, everything was pretty normal with them.

Lennon listened, then said, "I'd say we have three or four minutes. Time to make one more drop. The next ledge is only about eight feet down."

Crystal fell to her knees. "I've lost my will to live. Leave me and save yourselves."

Ashley rolled her eyes and tapped her friend with a foot. "You first this time, Crystal. Let's move it."

The process was repeated. Finally, only Ashley remained. Above her head, she heard the scrabble of boots on the hard surface.

Ashley expected to see bearded faces peering down at her from the cliff top. Instead, high-pitched screams resonated from the walls of her ledge. She clutched her ears as two bodies hurtled past, so close she could have reached out and touched them. Arms and legs flailed in a vain attempt to cheat gravity. Two of the loggers had been fooled into thinking they were stepping onto a solid field of rock.

Plop. Thud. The bodies landed on the narrow rock beach at the bottom of the crater. The screams stopped.

Ashley flattened against the cliff and waited for more bodies to fall.

A rough voice shouted, "Lonnie and Jeff went right off the edge. Everybody stand back. There's a freaking drop-off."

Another man responded, "I'm going to look over and see how far down it is. Maybe they're still alive. Hang onto my belt."

Ashley, come on. We're out of time.

Lennon's words didn't come from below. Did she just hear his voice in her mind? She smacked the side of her head with a fist. Okay, maybe thought transference was normal in this enchanted world.

I know, she thought back, hoping it worked both ways. *They might see me if I drop.*

Doesn't matter. Hurry."

Uh-huh, thought transference, definitely. Creepy but kind of awesome.

The second man said, "Nope. They aren't moving. Nobody can survive a fall like that. Must be 75, 80 feet down."

"Where'd them kids go, then?"

"Don't know. I only see Lonnie and Jeff. Their necks are twisted and there's lots of blood on the rocks around them. They just missed the water."

"Why don't we just leave the kids and go back to camp? They'll probably die out here anyway."

"Can't take the chance they make it back and squeal on us. We're facing jail time if we're caught taking the big trees without a license."

Ashley couldn't wait any longer. If the loggers moved around the perimeter of the crater, looking for signs of their prey, would they be able to see them on the ledges? The men could have re-loaded their guns. She'd rather die with her friends than here by herself.

Her body slid over the side of the cliff and Lennon pulled her in.

A voice shouted. "I just seen one a them kids. Must be some kind of shelf underneath."

While angry voices bellowed overhead, the four teens huddled together as close to the wall as possible.

"We can't stay here," Lennon whispered to the girls. "The loggers will realize if we got down, they can too. There are nine men left. And, this is the last ledge. Nothing under us but the rocks rimming the lake." His eyes morphed from their normal deep blue to a hard, fathomless black, reminding Ashley that the plague virus might have changed him in a way she didn't fully understand.

"Observation here." Crystal's voice quavered. "This is a lose-lose for us. We can throw ourselves to our doom and save the loggers the bother. That's about the only option."

"I got nothing to suggest." Ashley looked at Lennon. "Now would be a good time to show us what *you* got. Mystical invisibility spell, heavenly miracle, transcendence, magic carpet? Anything?"

Lennon ran his tongue over his newly filed eyeteeth. If they lived another day, Ashley was going to tell him to knock it off. His fangs were gone. Gone forever, and just get over it already.

He avoided Ashley's scrutiny. Picking up one backpack at a time, he held it over the ledge, lined up a spot below, and dropped it. Ashley and her friends watched this operation without complaint. What use were cell phones and winter jackets when you were dead?

When the last pack disappeared from sight, Lennon looked over his shoulder at Ashley. "This ledge is more or less 25 feet from the ground."

"The lake is surrounded by a rock shore, not soft, sandy beach." Ashley recognised the paralysis of fear overtaking her brain. She knew she was incapable of rational thought, because she was totally open to Lennon telling them why it was okay to jump from the ledge to certain death.

Lennon continued as though she hadn't spoken. "If we take a running jump off this ledge, we should clear the rock beach directly below and the ... um ... bodies, and hit the water. I don't know for sure we'll make it and I don't know how deep the lake is. Staying here, we'll die for sure. Jumping, we have a chance."

"A teeny-tiny chance," Jane mumbled.

Curses rumbled down at them, as the loggers

prepared to descend to the first ledge above their heads. Ashley hoped at least a few of them joined their buddies on the floor of the crater. Shouldn't she feel guilty about that hope? Maybe, but she didn't. Her team was greatly outnumbered and any mishap to the baddies wouldn't keep her up nights.

"I'll go first," Lennon said. "When I surface, I'll wave my arm, and another one jump. Do it alone. Trying to do it together will shorten your run time."

Ashley clutched his arm. "Say we all make it into the lake. What will stop those men from doing the same thing?"

He wrenched himself free. Feet first, he soared into the void.

CHAPTER 25

LENNON USED A SHOT OF super strength to increase his trajectory in case the water was shallow at the edges. He landed with a splash near the centre of the lake. After a few seconds of free fall through the murky depths, he broke for the surface. The water was pleasantly tepid, not frigid as he expected from a meteor lake.

He bobbed to the surface, swiping water from his eyes, searching for the girls. They remained in the overhanging gloom of the second and last ledge.

He beckoned to them with one hand, holding the index finger of his other hand straight up as he treaded water with his legs. If they leaped together, they would fall on the two bodies lying on the narrow rocky beach.

On the cliff top, three men formed a chain to

lower a fourth onto the first ledge, his red-checkered shirt bright against the grey rock of the crater. The girls were arguing, probably Ashley urging Crystal to jump. He waved at them again, knowing he was drawing attention to himself.

One of the men, not engaged in the chain operation, pulled his weapon out and fired at Lennon. So, good to know there were still bullets they had to dodge. A couple of others fired as well. Lennon watched the bullets cleave the water a few metres away. He waved frantically at the girls again.

The man at the end of the chain let go too soon. Instead of landing on the first ledge above the girls, he dropped straight down, shrieking for help. Lennon heard the thud as the man hit the rocky beach. His body half rolled until his head was underwater, rivulets of blood staining the rocks. Now, there were eight.

Crystal backed against the rock wall and Lennon figured she was too petrified to chance it. But he had to give her credit. She always came through in the end. With falling bodies and gunshots directly above her head, she ran straight out into space. She was going to clear the rim of stone, but was on a path to land only ten or twelve feet inside the water line. Lennon couldn't tell if the depth there was safe.

In the months since he had been cured, he played around with moving small objects by using hand movements and his mind. Would the ability work with a human body? With his legs churning the lukewarm water, he held up his right hand, palm out, and willed Crystal's body to move toward him.

Crystal's eyes were closed and she chanted, "Oh god, oh god," over and over as she plummeted. But, when she should have plunged into the water only yards from the third dead man's immersed head, she jerked to a halt like she'd hit a closed door, then sailed in a straight line towards Lennon. He ducked under the water to absorb the impact of her body landing on him. He disentangled her from his neck and hauled her up.

Leaving her to sputter and tread in place, he beckoned for the next girl. With a wild battle cry, Jane hurtled toward him. Good try, but she was going to fall short. This time, he was able to control speed and drop-down point. Jane entered the water gently and bobbed back up in a few seconds.

"What a ride!" she shouted. "Come on, Ashley, you've got nothing to lose."

Ashley screamed words that Lennon was never allowed to say in his foster homes. To hear them come out of Ashley's mouth was kind of a shock as he waited for her to run head-long off the ledge. Not waiting to see where she would land, he used his "magnet" hand to pull her over. He planned to drop her as gently as Jane, but the expression of fury on her face reminded him of the days she used to scare the crap out of him. He lost his focus. She went in head first and disappeared.

He dived and searched for her. He wasn't sure how far down he swam before catching sight of her blonde ponytail swaying slowly in the still water.

Taking firm hold of the ponytail with one hand and her back holster with the other, he kicked his feet and headed back up. He broke the surface first, then raised her face to the open air. She coughed and kicked at him. His sense of relief overcame his normal reserve — he pulled her face towards his and kissed her on the lips.

Ashley swatted at his head, her closed fist making his ear ring. "What's the matter with you? First, you almost drown me, then you plant your lips on me. Chill out!"

"Sorry, I ..."

"Wait." Ashley looked at him. "What did you do? I was pulled out like I was on a bungee cord. Was that you?"

"He did it to us, too," Crystal said. "And, those assholes are still firing at us, and we can't tread water forever."

Jane's sodden, red spikes drooped over her forehead. "What do we do, now? Lennon, you said you have a plan. I hope it includes moving to dry land soon because I don't want to tangle with giant water snakes or flesh-eating plants."

"I'm swimming for shore," Crystal announced. The brief plunge underwater had finished the process of unwinding her braids and plastered strands of long, black hair against her skull. "I'll have a heart attack right here if I see a snake."

"We're in more danger from bacteria than snakes," Ashley offered, throwing Lennon an unreadable look. "This water is murky, and I swallowed a gallon. No telling what microbes are swimming around in my body now."

Like the water quality was his fault? Lennon spoke up before he had a mutiny on his hands. "We *are* heading for shore, but to our right towards the waterfall."

"Explain your plan," Ashley said. "This trip has turned out a whole lot different than *I planned*. You got us into this; maybe you can get us out."

Lennon swam a few feet away from her. "There's a cave or tunnel behind the waterfall. I can see it from here."

"Well, we can't. How do you know it isn't just a blind cave with no way out?" Ashley whipped her drenched ponytail, flinging water into his face. Not that he wasn't wet already, but, sheesh. He couldn't tell them that, when they first stumbled on the crater, he saw a couple of First Nations spectres slip behind the waterfall. Sure, maybe the early peoples used the space for storage and it didn't lead anywhere, but they hadn't any choice other than to check it out.

"We'll come up on the waterfall on the side away

from the loggers. We have to get there fast before they realize what we're up to. Right now, we have a few minutes until they figure out how to get to us, but if they stand where the river pours over the cliff, they might be close enough to shoot us."

"Listen," Ashley said, "I'm not leaving my backpack behind. It's got my phone and my jacket, and lot of other important stuff."

"Once you're hidden behind the waterfall, I'll get our packs. It'll take me about 10 seconds." He'd switch to super speed and with any luck, the loggers wouldn't think to shoot at a blur of colour.

Ashley swam ahead of Lennon in the water. "Let's do it. I've always wanted to see the back of a waterfall."

Lennon knew she really didn't, and he promised himself he would stand well back from her if the cave behind the waterfall was a dead end. He was out of ideas, and the cave would become their tomb.

CHAPTER 26

ASHLEY SWAM TOWARD THE WATERFALL while the loggers ran parallel along the cliff ridge — but not close enough to slip over, dammit. Ashley kicked faster. She pulled ahead of her friends, annoyed when Lennon passed her and crawled over the slippery rocks where the spray was heaviest. Not that she could get any wetter, and the spray afforded some cover from overhead.

She let Lennon take her hand and haul her out, while he motioned to the space between the falling water and the cliff behind. She held her breath and ducked through the wall of tumbling water. Panic overwhelmed her as the weight of the waterfall forced her to her knees. She didn't dare take a breath, afraid she would drown for sure.

Hands pushed on her butt and shoved her clear.

Ashley brushed water from her eyes and looked around a narrow grotto, slick with moisture. Anyone else for claustrophobia?

A black void gaped in the centre of the rock wall. Slightly dizzy, Ashley dropped to her hands and knees. She crawled close to the wall to give her friends some room. The drop-off to the tumble of rocks below wasn't deep, but if one of them slipped off, they could suffer a broken leg or a concussion before being swept back into the lake. Game over.

As Crystal and Jane joined her, then Lennon, they found it impossible to talk or hear over the roar of falling water. Lennon edged past Ashley and stuck his head through the torrent of water.

He held up a finger, a signal Ashley didn't understand and wished he would stop using, before he was gone in a blaze of motion. She looked over her shoulder to make sure her friends were okay and received a thumbs-up from both. Awesome. More digit signs. At least she understood thumbs.

A momentary break in the waterfall announced Lennon's return. He carried two backpacks in each hand. His dripping tee shirt clung to his body, outlining the lean muscles of his chest. Ashley shook the wet hair from her eyes and tried to find someplace else to look. The black gash of the cave opening caught her focus and made her heart rate and breathing accelerate.

Her dagger rested in its harness so she didn't need

to root through her pack to unwrap the weapon like the others. She slipped the dagger free and examined the blade. Sharp, but not much protection against bullets. Or, against whatever waited for them if the cave led to a tunnel unused for centuries.

On her knees for stability, Jane scooped up a handful of water from the waterfall and drank. The others watched and, when she didn't keel over dead, did the same. Ashley drank as much as she could, hoping to fool her stomach into thinking it was full of solid food, but that didn't work. She could feel the rumbling, even if she couldn't hear it.

She considered pulling out her phone and trying to call for help. Waste of time. In this cursed place, which maybe wasn't even real, there would be zero bars. No one was coming to their rescue. Holding her dagger against her thigh, she waited for the others.

Thirst quenched, weapons ready, the four turned to face the cleft in the cliff wall. An overpowering urge to take the lead swept over Ashley. She elbowed Lennon aside and thrust her free hand into the emptiness beyond the dark.

Time to stop being such a complete and utter wuss.

CHAPTER 27

WHAT THE HELL? LENNON CLUTCHED the back of Ashley's tee shirt. He pulled her back and inserted himself into the space. This wasn't a blank wall. Maybe it would end in a storage cavern, but they couldn't stay here.

He was aware that Ashley didn't like closed-in spaces. Making her walk behind him with her friends at her back caused her anxiety to spike, but he couldn't let her take the lead. His fingers encircled Ashley's wrist, hoping she got the message to form a chain like they did during their earlier flights through the forest.

When he sensed they were connected and no one would be left behind, he proceeded, step by careful step. He held his curved knife straight out in front of him so it — and not his face — would come in contact with *anything* solid in his path. "Nobody turn on a phone or flashlight. We can't chance being seen from behind."

Even his enhanced vision needed some light to allow his pupils to expand, and there was no light source here. He had his hearing, though, and he was better able to distinguish an animal or human threat than Ashley. If anything breathed within fifty yards, he'd hear it.

Cautiously, he reached out to her with his mind to explain, and was rewarded with a *Bite me!* Okay, then, telepathy working just fine. Why could he perceive Ashley's thoughts or transmit his to her, but not to Crystal or Jane? He hadn't really tried with them, though.

They plodded along the uneven stone floor of the tunnel. It was cold and damp, and he felt Ashley's fingers tremble in his. There was no room to stop and put on warmer, dry clothes, even if men with guns weren't right on their asses.

His shoulders brushed the rough walls and, when he reached up with his knife, he figured he had about two inches of clearance. Kind of tight. Bug feet scuttled along the walls ahead of him, and he was relieved the river running overhead blocked the faint sound from the girls' ears. With any luck, they wouldn't notice the soft rustlings overhead. This was no place for an epic Crystal meltdown.

Ahead, a pinpoint of greenish light approached and, as they moved forward, it filled the blackness.

Freaking wonderful. The green glow became human-shaped as it bobbed closer. Would this be a spectre that walked in another dimension, or would it be interactive like the railway worker who locked eyes with Lennon and tried to hit on Ashley?

The ghost's clothing was similar to that worn by the First Nations man he had glimpsed from the ridge of the crater. The spectre didn't appear aware of their presence which was a bonus.

Lennon noted with dread that the spectre was not alone. The light was too encompassing to be released by just one. So far, he had been able to step aside when approached by a remnant and didn't know what direct impact would do to him. To avoid eye contact, he turned his head to the slimy wall of the tunnel and watched an iridescent insect crawl into a crevice. He braced himself.

An icy ball tore through his chest as the lead ancient First Nations man walked right through the line of living teens. A second passed through, then a third. Each time, the chill in his body increased. Shards of ice encircled his heart.

Lennon looked over his shoulder. The spectre-light allowed him to see Ashley's eyes widen in shock. Crystal looked uneasy. He couldn't see the shorter Jane at the back of the line but assumed her reaction probably matched Crystal's.

The iciness passed gradually, leaving the sensation of a load of bricks in his stomach. He shuddered, hoping he wouldn't encounter any more spectres in this place where it was impossible to move out of their way.

He might have to explain a few things to Ashley later. For some reason, she sensed ghosts but didn't see them. He tugged on her fingers and they set off again, the tunnel floor abruptly changing from level ground to a steep incline.

The thunder of the river faded gradually as they made their way uphill. He heard Jane complaining that her freaking hatchet had ripped a hole in her jeans. Apparently, talking was possible again.

Lennon avoided Ashley's eyes which flashed blue fire in the darkness. Weird. "We've been heading up for a while. The tunnel is narrowing and the ceiling getting lower. We may have to start crawling soon. I think we're close to the surface."

"We don't know if something is blocking the exit." Crystal huffed as she sucked air into her lungs. "Kind of moldy in here, don't you think? Between microbes from the lake and mold in this tunnel, we don't have a shot in hell of surviving this magical quest. Good thing we don't have to find a fiery cauldron to throw a gold ring into."

"Quit being drastic for once, Crystal," Jane retorted. "I have a rip in my best jeans the size of K.K.'s ass. I'm slimy with whatever is on these walls. If it's mold, its *rotted* mold. Let's just go find this possibly-blocked exit and get out of here."

Ashley hadn't uttered a sound, which made Lennon nervous and, when he got nervous, he babbled. "So, then, if I drop your hand, Ashley, that's a signal that I'm crawling and everyone should do the same. I'll try to go slow, so we won't leave anyone behind ..."

Ashley worked her wrist free of his grip. The skin on her arm brushed against his cheek as she pointed ahead. "Is that daylight?"

CHAPTER 28

NO WONDER ASHLEY'S EYES SHONE in the dark. The pinpoint of light ahead reflected off her blue irises. Lennon was thankful he hadn't mentioned it to her, imagining her scornful eye roll. The heat of embarrassment crept up his neck, actually a comfort after the chill of three ghosts marching through his guts. He should have noticed the light before Ashley.

The point of light could be a hundred feet away, or ten. If ten, they were screwed because that meant the exit was blocked. They could deal with vegetation, but if centuries of tremblers from the shifting tectonic plates offshore had rolled heavy boulders against the ancient entrance to the tunnel, they had no choice but to retrace their steps back to the waterfall and hope the loggers had given up the chase. As if. He would hear them if they were in the tunnel already, but that didn't mean they hadn't descended into the crater and would find the tunnel any second. Fleetingly, he recalled the warring robed figures and ninja-types. They were out there somewhere, too.

"Well, are you going to move towards the light or not?" Ashley snapped.

The other girls snickered, and Lennon resisted the urge to tell them that the afterlife was a little more complicated than most people thought. Instead, he moved forward again, this time leaving the others to follow on their own.

The tiny circle of light grew in size and became a rough oval. Hopelessness rolled over him the closer he got. The ancient peoples must have been smaller in stature because no way would his shoulders fit through the opening. Jane was the smallest. Maybe he could shove her out first.

Ashley's finger drilled into his back. "Move it. I want to take my last breath in sunlight, not in this horrible hell's armpit."

Lennon opened his mouth to tell her they were too big to fit, but the words never left his mouth. He used his enhanced sight and realized trees had grown around the exit. Branches of seedling firs swept across the opening. He could tear them out by the roots if he had to. It would still be a squeeze for him, but the girls shouldn't have a problem.

"Let me look first," he told them. Bracing his legs

and pushing one hand against the rough stone walls of the tunnel, he thrust his head out.

Sunlight. Summer warmth. In the distance, the hoarse cries of ravens, and the thundering of the river. He scanned left to right. Trees everywhere, with no sign of the rocky field leading to the crater. Reaching out with his mind, he detected no presence. At least, no human presence.

Ahead, the unearthly glow of a half dozen first peoples sat around a campfire, roasting their meal over green flames. Several small children ran through the trees — literally, through the trees — their mouths open in silent squeals of pleasure. Lennon preferred to believe they had come back to their special place of contentment and peace after death. It was too sad to think that they died here violently while living their everyday lives.

"How's it looking out there?" Ashley's voice broke through his musing. Well, her voice and the finger in his back.

Without answering, he used his knife to hack off the branches that obscured the opening. He had to get out first, or nobody was getting out. The tunnel here had narrowed to the point where his shoulders brushed the walls and it would be impossible for any of the girls to get past him.

When the whole of the rock exit was revealed, Lennon's stomach tightened around the load of bricks again. He would never fit.

"What's the holdup?" Jane called. "I'm getting itchy in here."

"That would be the mold spores attaching to your skin before boring into your bloodstream," Crystal answered. "We're goners."

Anything was better than listening to this. "Hold my knife for me, will you?" Lennon handed his weapon and backpack to Ashley. Turning his body sideways, he shoved one arm through. His head and shoulder followed, and that was as far as he could go. He was stuck.

A pair of arms lifted his legs and shoved. He scrunched his trapped shoulder towards his chest, sure his torso would be crushed. Then, like Superman, he shot from the hole with one arm extended, and the other against his side.

Okay, he didn't exactly fly out, but once both arms were free, he was able to wiggle the rest of his body out. He lay on the warm ground and panted. Looking up, he caught the interested glance of one of the elders sitting around the campfire. The elder inclined his head. Lennon nodded back before quickly looking away. What the hell?

His backpack flew from the hole and hit him on the ankle. He stepped back as three more followed. "A little help, please," Ashley called. Her arms protruded from the tunnel's mouth, flapping wildly, and one hand flourished his knife.

Lennon retrieved his weapon and pulled the

girls out. While they flopped on the ground moaning about hunger and thirst, he extended his hearing range to its max, blocking out the girls' voices and the distant pounding of the river as it plummeted over the rim of the crater.

Underneath the natural sounds, he recognized a faint vibration in the earth as human footfalls, light ones, still a distance away. If his senses weren't screwed up by enchantments, he'd place it at least a mile away. The math wasn't reassuring. Where was Hank right now? Was he still lost and looking for his family? Lennon wrenched his thoughts from that path.

He jumped when Ashley spoke close to his ear. "Any ideas?"

He hadn't. Not one. "Several people are headed our way through the forest from left of the crater." He glanced across at the elder who lifted his head and held up one hand, waiting. When Lennon met his gaze, the elder pointed in the direction of the thundering river. Was that north? Lennon looked up, locating the sun through the tree canopy, thinking he could use its position to calculate direction.

"That's not good," he said. "It must be hours since we found the clearing with the crater. Remember, the sun was directly overhead." He pointed up. "It still is."

Under a layer of grime, Ashley's face paled. "I

hate this forest. Something is screwing with climate and time. It could be Monday already."

Jane intoned, "In the year 2042, the skeletal remains of four teenagers were found in a remote forested area of Vancouver Island. The cause of death could not be determined." Her index finger moved back and forth, then pointed. "No, seriously, I vote we head towards the river. I can hear it."

Crystal picked up her hammer and stood. "We could get drinking water there, and maybe back-trace to the train tracks." She had her phone out and held it skyward, turning in a circle. "Nada."

Ashley threw her friends a disgusted look. "We were already lost when we found the crater."

"Hold it down for a minute," Lennon directed.

Flattening himself on the ground, he dropped his head into the tunnel and concentrated. He jerked back and leaped to his feet. "Come on, we need to get away from here fast. More people are running through the tunnel. Their footsteps are light, like the ones coming at us through the forest. Not the loggers."

"Like ninjas or the cloaked people? So, we got baddies coming at us from the tunnel and from the forest?" Ashley drew her dagger and swung her pack across her shoulders "Which way?"

"Wait a minute," Crystal said. "We know the loggers want to kill us. But, we don't know the intentions of the cloaks and ninjas. One of those two groups might help us."

Jane pulled a cobweb from the tangle of Crystal's long hair. "Yeah, but which group? Just because they were fighting each other, doesn't mean one of them is going to buy us ice cream before driving us home in their Cadillac Escalade with reclining seats."

"We trust no one!" Ashley countered. She turned to Lennon. "Are we moving out, or waiting here to be captured and murdered?"

If only Lennon knew the location of the loggers. He couldn't hear the heavily-booted, rifle-toting outdoorsmen, but they had to be close by, too. Maybe they were standing around, either lost or waiting to ambush the teens, unaware the other two groups were closing in. With any luck, though, the loggers had given up the chase and returned to camp. If they could find it.

Lennon led them away from the sound of the river, away from the direction indicated by the elder spectre. In his view, the departed were no more trustworthy than the living. The spectre could send them into a trap. The loggers' motive was clear — they wanted their illegal operation to remain secret. What about the ninja guys and the cloaked ones? Somebody was after him, Lennon couldn't deny that, but who? And, why?

Lennon and the girls had to stay out of the grasp of all hunters until they escaped this unnatural forest and could figure out the reason for all this. Right

now, they were in a life and death situation. They
had to keep running.

CHAPTER 29

ASHLEY REMEMBERED HER MOTHER TELLING her not to run with a stick. That seemed such a long, long time ago. And here she was, running with a dagger through a tropical rainforest in January on Vancouver Island while sweating buckets and catching occasional glimpses of a sun that wouldn't set.

She was responsible for placing her friends in danger. Whatever brain fart made her think this trek was a good idea would probably end very badly. Like, in death. If she hadn't insisted on coming along, Lennon would be able to use his super speed and outrun their pursuers. Except he'd be alone.

She looked back to make sure her friends were close, smacking into Lennon who had stopped again. Not that they couldn't use a break.

"Shht." Lennon tipped his head up, like a wolf. Ashley would give anything for super hearing. Or, any one of his powers.

"They're catching up." He looked upwards at the trees that soared as high as a three-story building. "We have to go up."

Jane and Crystal leaned against nearby trunks, breathing heavily. Their weapons hung from limp fingers. Random slivers of light sliced through the green canopy, throwing pale shadows across their grimy faces.

Ashley's instincts demanded she turn and fight. They might die, but she would rather go down fighting hand-to-hand than be picked off from a tree branch by whatever weapons the enemy would wield. "These spruces are taller than Vic High. We can't even reach the lower branches. You climb up, Lennon, and cover us. We'll fight on the ground."

In answer, Lennon picked up Jane and pitched her upward. Jane caught a thick branch and swung her leg over.

"Shitballs, super-boy, I almost took my ear off with my hatchet."

"Climb," Lennon urged. When Jane had ascended a couple of feet, he tossed Crystal up. She missed the first time, and he tried again. She wrapped her leg around the branch and pulled the rest of her body to safety. At least her meat-tenderizing hammer wouldn't slice off a body part.

The spruce branches snapped back in place as she disappeared from view.

Ashley stood close to the trunk. "Lift me to your shoulders. I can reach the branch from there." No way did she want to be tossed like a soccer ball. She placed the hilt of her dagger between her teeth to free up her hands.

Balancing on Lennon's shoulders, Ashley jumped and caught the lowest branch. Swinging her leg, she strained to get her ankle over. Lennon jumped onto the branch and hauled her the rest of the way. So much for being independent.

He whispered to Ashley. "See if you can get higher than Jane. I'll stay down here. That way we can keep the girls between us."

"How much time do we have?"

"A minute, maybe two."

She might have a bit of trouble with confined spaces like the tunnel, but she wasn't afraid of heights. Ashley climbed past Crystal and Jane who clung to the trunk like tree frogs. She squeezed each shoulder, hoping to reassure her friends, but neither met her eyes. Yeah, she knew this was her doing. She should have left them at home.

She settled on a thick branch, her feet nearly touching Jane's head. She must be fifty feet up.

She wrapped her arms around the rough bark of the trunk and waited for the inevitable discovery. They had been stalked unerringly so far. What were chances the trackers wouldn't realize the path of their prey ended at the base of this tree?

Her head snapped up. There was a rustling in the thick spruce needles above. What lived in trees here? They had seen no creatures in this strange forest unless you counted the white ravens, and where were they when you needed them?

The rustling grew louder. Jane and Crystal looked up.

"Don't worry about it. Just a bird or something."

Jane pointed above Ashley's head and her eyes grew wide. Crystal's inevitable, 'oh god, oh god' drew Lennon's attention. "Quiet, they're almost here."

One of the hardest things Ashley had to do so far on this doomed journey was look upwards into the branches.

A pair of golden eyes surrounded by pale brown fur blinked at her.

Startled, Ashley's grip on the trunk loosened. As she began to topple, a heavy, hairy arm reached down and shoved her back against the tree.

Ashley pressed her face against the bark. "Thanks, Hank."

Glancing up, Lennon said, "That's not Hank."

CHAPTER 30

FOOTSTEPS ADVANCED SILENTLY AND RAPIDLY through the forest like a trained militia. With his eyesight turned up full throttle, Lennon waited for them to come into view. Which group would it be?

He didn't have long to wait. When he spied the first figure, he called to Ashley's mind. *It's the four ninja-looking guys. They're almost here. Everyone stay quiet and I'll see what they want. Tell the others.*

He preferred to face the advancing threat to dealing with Ashley who was nose to nose with a Hank-like being. He hadn't a clue why these men were after him, or even if they were the same ones who had been tailing his every move for the past few months. He decided to stay on his branch.

As the first man advanced, Lennon muted his vision to near-normal. Three others remained draped in shadows before a signal from the leader brought them forward to surround the base of the tree harbouring the four teens. How did the ninjas know which tree out of a million to focus on?

The four men were slightly built and didn't carry visible weapons, unlike the loggers. But, they were even more terrifying. Clad entirely in form-fitting black, their heads and faces were wrapped with only slits in the cloth for their eyes and mouths. Lennon switched back to enhanced vision and gave each set of eyes a quick scan. Two brown, one blue, one grey. Nothing unusual about their lips, either. He couldn't tell the skin or hair colour. One pair of brown eyes looked familiar, in a foggy kind of way, like from a long-ago dream. If only this whole trip was a dream.

He decided on a pre-emptive move. "What can I do for you guys? Are you lost, too?" A tight fist of terror clenched his heart, but his casual comment masked his fear. He hoped.

The dude with the familiar dark eyes replied, "You're coming with us." His rumbling words sounded like he was disguising his voice, not at all menacing unless you had super hearing and could sense the threatening undertone. "The blonde girl, too. The others can stay where they are until we leave."

Had he heard that voice before? "Why do you

want us?"

"It's government business. We think you can help us with further studies on the virus that infected the residents of the Island a few months back."

"You'll have to do better than that."

One of the figures leaned over and whispered into the spokesman's ear. They appeared to argue for a minute before the first guy said, "If you all come down now, we'll make sure the other two girls get home safely."

Why would they want Ashley? She hadn't been infected with the virus. Nope. "Nobody's coming down from the tree. How'd you track us anyway?"

The talking ninja ignored the question. "Then we'll have to come up and get you. We have Tasers. We don't want to use them, but we will if necessary."

"Nope." How were they going to get out of this one? Hand weapons were no match for Tasers and trained fighters.

The four men consulted, then the first one spoke again. "All right. Have it your way. I'm coming up and my colleagues will try and catch each of you when you fall. We'll see how that goes."

Lennon climbed higher and nudged Crystal. "Move up. We won't make this easy for them."

As soon as Jane and Ashley were at the same level, he crouched on a branch opposite Crystal's. The Sasquatch had disappeared from sight. Had it leaped to another tree?

Ashley's voice reached his ears. "Jane and Crystal, you have a choice. They don't want you. But, I'm not going with them without a fight. Looks like Lennon has a choice to make, too."

"I fight," Lennon's answered, his words ringing with resolve.

"I don't trust them. I don't believe they work for the government," Crystal said. "I'm staying right here. If one of them tries to grab me, I'll smash his fingers to mush with my hammer."

"Ditto on the violence to baddies," Jane responded. "I think a hatchet to the forehead might slow one down."

Ashley swung her dagger, slicing off a small branch that bounced off Lennon's head. "Okay, looks like we fight. A threat to one of us is a threat to all."

"One thing, though." Crystal's voice wasn't quite as strong as before. "You guys remember what we talked about when the bikers had us cornered in Ross Bay Cemetery last October? If things go bad here, which star will we meet up on?"

"First star past the Milky Way," Jane replied. "You, too, Lennon."

Lennon enjoyed a fleeting sense of acceptance before the man spoke again.

"Time's up, kids. What's the decision?"

"Guess you'll have to come get us," Lennon told the ninjas. There was a first time for everything, like smoking pot or getting tased. He was curious about the first, but not looking forward to the second.

"Everyone pull your feet up under you," Ashley ordered. "No dangling."

The head ninja called up, "Okay, I lied. We don't have Tasers. We have something better, and you'll like it even less."

Sighting down the line of the trunk to the ground, Lennon noticed one of the ninjas place both hands on the trunk of the tree. A small black box lay under one of his hands. He leaned forward, pressing the box into the bark.

The branch quivered under Lennon's feet. This had to be some form of energy distortion. He wrapped his arms around the trunk and yelled to the girls, "Hang on."

The ninja pressed his hands harder against the trunk, and the tree pulsated from roots to crown. The spruce convulsed more and more violently as though trying to dislodge every needle from its branches.

Jane flew off her branch, followed by Crystal and Ashley. Lennon held on as long as possible, but the powerful motion made him dizzy. His arms were wrenched from the trunk and he tumbled backward.

The heavy body of Hank's lookalike fell from the upper branches and passed Lennon as they plummeted towards the ground. The creature must have been up there all along.

Lennon had time to be afraid and think about death and how much he would miss the girls, especially Ashley, which made no sense.

He was inches from the ground when his body jerked up and down as if a giant was bouncing him at the end of an elastic band. When he stopped bouncing, he dropped face first to the ground. Unhurt, he rolled over on his back. Before he could sit up, a black-clad figure loomed over him pointing a weapon at his chest.

Here it comes. He hoped he didn't pee himself when the jolt of electricity hit his body.

He fell into black nothingness.

CHAPTER 31

ASHLEY'S INSTINCTS TOLD HER TO keep her eyes closed. She had woken up a few minutes ago, remembering the fall from the tree but, strangely, no impact. A ninja had pointed a weapon at her and that was the last she knew until now.

She was tied down or the jostling would have thrown her off this thing she was lying on. Stretcher?

"How much farther we got to go?" a man asked. He spoke with a heavy accent. Maybe East European?

"Some distance yet. Sergei will hover the copter above the logging camp. Tree trunks too numerous to land. These assets will be hauled up by ropes and delivered to the lab." This guy sounded Italian or Spanish. "Too bad that strange monkey ran off before we could send him to dreamland, too. I'm guessing we'd get a bonus for that one."

"What about us? I've had enough of this place. What kind of a forest is it where there's no animals or birds except a funny ape and white crows? And, that protection ward we ran into — good thing it was weakening or we never would have broken through."

Good old Canadian accent on this one, maybe East Coast. The fourth man, one of Lennon's captors, hadn't spoken.

"We make our own way out, and hope not to run into Keepers again. Also, we do not mention loggers to Command. Not kidding. We better hope nobody finds those bodies until they're good and rotted."

A chorus of voices agreed with that plan. Ashley waited to hear them mention Crystal and Jane, but the men fell silent and the bumpy journey continued.

Lennon was nearby. She sensed he was conscious. She sent out a thought strand.

What's happening? Where's Jane and Crystal?

I don't know about them. They're taking us to some lab. Keep your eyes closed.

I'm tied down. How are we going to get away? Can you use your super strength to break free?

Not right now. Whatever they used to knock us out has weakened me. Don't know how long it will last. They used heavy twine, not rope, so it should be easy for me to break it if I regain my strength in time.

This was it, then. They were doomed. Her friends were probably already dead. This obviously had something to do with the LM43 virus, or they wouldn't be after Lennon. Maybe he wasn't the only victim to retain enhanced abilities. Why did they want her? The only thing different about her was the mind-thing with Lennon, and nobody knew about that — she hadn't even had time to share it with her two best friends. Gee-zuz, Crystal and Jane just couldn't be dead.

Ashley's head banged against a tree trunk, and the pain radiated down her body. It was hard to keep from crying out, and harder to keep her eyes closed.

The guy with the European accent laughed cruelly. "Oops, sorry girly. That a big bump. Good thing she still out cold."

"Let's hope they stay that way until we hand them off. I don't want to have to deal with a lot of screaming."

The others snorted agreement. Ashley imagined the hilt of her dagger smashing against the teeth of these jerks. Fury coursed through her blood, and she had to fight to keep her eyes shut. Truthfully, chances were small she'd ever see the dagger again. It had flown out of her hand as she fell from the tree. She couldn't think of her friends again right now.

The throbbing pain in her head took her mind off the discomfort in her shoulders. These creeps hadn't taken the time to rip off her empty holster before tying her down, and the leather dug into her flesh.

Her eyes almost popped open as she remembered something. Could it still be there? The ninjas had wrapped the twine over and around the stretcher with her arms bound tightly to her body. Except, the twine had loosened with all the jostling.

Inch by inch, Ashley slid her right hand under her butt and searched for the object in her back pocket. Disappointed, she found her tube of lip gloss, then ... Hah! A longer, flatter object.

She froze as the goon carrying her foot-end said to his buddy. "Got to take leak. Be back." He dropped the stretcher and Ashley's body slid down until her heels made contact with the ground. He didn't notice and she heard him move away a few steps. Hope he turned his back, the pig.

The guy at her head dropped his load, the impact sending another arrow of pain through her head. He called to the ninjas carrying Lennon's stretcher, "Break time."

This was their chance. Ashley shifted her weight from the stretcher. With her thumb and index finger, she edged the switchblade out of her pocket. Locating the button, she pushed it and the blade shot out. She worked it against the strand of twine near her hand

and felt it separate.

She lay still for a moment, until she was sure neither man standing nearby had noticed her movements. In the distance, the boisterous croak of a raven called, and was answered by another.

"You hearing crows again? Something is peculiar about white crows."

"What's peculiar is they're the only birds in the forest. No animals either."

"I never come back to this place. Something wrong here. Not just Keepers." The sound of a sliding zipper announced that break time was almost over.

Ashley took advantage of her litter-bearers' distraction over the "crows" to saw through the binding at her hip level. The blade was razor sharp. In seconds, the lower half of her body was free. If any of them looked at her, they wouldn't miss the pieces of twine scattered across her legs.

Ashley sent out another thought to Lennon.

Have a blade in my back pocket. Hacked through some of the twine but positive it will be noticed any second.

I'm getting stronger. Almost ready. We have to escape before we reach the logging camp. Be ready to go. I won't leave you.

Never mind me. If I can't get away, find Jane and Crystal.

The air turned chilly. They must be nearing the loggers' camp. From their earlier conversation, she believed the loggers were all dead, killed by these evil men. What freaking day was it? Maybe it was Monday and the supply train couldn't unload. Wouldn't the engineer contact his boss and initiate a search? That was such a long shot.

One of Lennon's stretcher carriers shouted, "I hear the chopper."

Ashley was freezing but didn't want to shiver and alert the ninjas that she was conscious. The constant jolting made her stomach queasy. Lucky there was nothing in it. She concentrated on not retching.

Lennon's mind reached out to hers, his thought unobtrusive, like the soft tickle of a kitten's paw.

I think I can do it now. Use your blade to slash, not stab. At the count of five, we go.

Ready.

She flexed her body to loosen the cord across her chest. She opened her eyes and for one awful moment, thought she was blind. When her vision adjusted, she realized the sun had finally set. It was winter again.

Five ...

Clutching the switchblade tightly, she cut through the last strands restraining her upper body. The man at her feet dropped the handles of the litter. "What the hell!"

Four ...

Sitting upright, Ashley quickly dealt with her leg bindings.

Three ...

Yelling at his companions to help, the man lunged at her. Ashley slashed the blade across his right wrist and then, without hesitation, the left. He shrieked with pain and backed away. The guy at her head dropped the handles and whirled around, reaching for her, all in one motion. These were trained fighters. They wouldn't be defeated for long.

Two ...

Ashley rolled off the stretcher and, from a kneeling position, swiped across the second man's chest, pressing the blade as hard as her strength allowed, hoping to open a cut deep enough to slow him down.

One ...

The fighter ignored his chest wound and grabbed her by the neck. His hands tightened. What the hell, one little stab couldn't hurt. She drove the blade into his thigh and twisted.

CHAPTER 32

LENNON SNAPPED HIS RESTRAINTS AND bounded from the portable stretcher. The two men carrying him had been alerted by Ashley's actions, and one tried to grab him. The other fumbled at his black-clad chest, hands searching. Taser? Gun?

Whatever. Lennon high-kicked, his heel smashing the man's hand into the weapon it was reaching for. He dealt the other man a stinging blow across the ear then drew back his foot and drove it into the man's ribs.

Ashley was on her feet, her two captors clutching various body parts and attempting to rise from their knees.

Throwing her over his shoulder, Lennon sped across the camp. Above, he heard the thunderous *whoomp-whoomp* of a hovering helicopter, and a powerful searchlight swept across the open area, lighting up the tents and log lean-to.

Still without his full super strength, Lennon struggled to carry Ashley and manoeuvre around the massive stumps while avoiding the searchlight. The four men who had captured them were not pursuing, not yet anyway. They had been caught off guard but wouldn't be so easy to defeat next time. Worse, more would come.

Lennon paused behind the lean-to and eased Ashley to the ground, feeling her shiver against his side. Taking in great gulps of air, he eyed the distance to the dark forest beyond the camp where the cloaked figures had emerged to tangle with the ninjas. What had happened to the cloaked ones? Were they out there, waiting for their turn to capture Lennon and Ashley? Or, were they dead like the loggers?

Leaning against the long building beside him were six semi-automatic rifles. He slid his fingers down the barrel of the nearest weapon until he found the safety lever, ensuring the safety switch was on.

"We can't leave these rifles here," he said to Ashley, quickly checking the levers of the other five. "Those guys will find them and use them on us. They weigh less than 10 pounds each. Can you carry two?"

"Uh, I guess. Just don't expect me to know how to use one. Hope I don't shoot my own face off."

"You can't. Not unless you switch off the safety lever. We have to get into the forest and hide."

He pointed up at the helicopter where a ladder was silhouetted against the residual glow of the searchlight. As they watched, a boot stepped onto the top rung, followed by the rest of a helmet-clad soldier with a weapon slung over one shoulder.

Lennon thrust two of the rifles into Ashley's arms and picked up the rest.

"This just keeps getter worse," Ashley moaned.

The searchlight swept over the hut again. As soon as it passed, Lennon said, "Okay, now we go."

They made it to the edge of the forest before the searchlight arced in their direction again. That didn't mean they weren't spotted by night vision goggles from inside the copter.

"They'll be after us in minutes." Lennon looked around until he found a rotted, moss-covered trunk. Feeling inside as far as he could reach, he looked up at Ashley. "We're going to hide the rifles in here."

He shoved his four inside the hollow log, flinching as he imagined the safety lever bumping against a protrusion and flipping to Fire. Lights out. He wrenched his mind from that thought and pushed hard to jam one of Ashley's rifles in after it.

"The last one won't fit." He laid it against the log and covered it with a layer of fallen pine needles. The enemy had bigger and more powerful weapons, but at least these six would never kill anyone.

He took Ashley's hand again. Her fingers were icy splinters. Not that his felt much warmer. He took a final look at the scene in the camp. "Those ninja guys aren't following us. Guess they have orders to leave us to the paramilitary dudes." He glanced up at the copter. "Freaking hell!"

"What?" Ashley jerked her hand from his and peered in the direction of the helicopter.

"They're lowering a dog. It can track us, no matter how far we run." Where was a friendly spectre with advice when you needed one? He was an idiot for ignoring the elder who had pointed him away from danger.

Heading deeper into the forest with Ashley in tow, he tried to get his bearings. "They'll be on the ground by now and tracking us. We'll circle around the camp and head back into the warded section of the forest."

Lennon knew Ashley would find fault with his plan and he was right.

"What good will that do? The ward has fallen. It's already getting colder in there and those ninjas can move freely in and out. Soldiers and dogs can follow us, too." Her teeth chattered so loudly, Lennon could hardly make out the words.

"Yeah, but it's still warmer than out here. And, daylight." He suspected the warded area had returned to normal time and climate already, but he didn't want Ashley to lose all hope.

"Do you remember when we last had a drink of water, or food? Who are those ninjas working for?

Do you think the soldiers are from our armed forces or are they mercenaries? Do you think we'll find Crystal and Jane before we die?"

Lennon chose to answer only one of her flood of questions. "The helicopter has no insignia identification, and I didn't see any shoulder flashings or badges on the soldiers. If they're from our government, they're conducting a black op."

One minute they were in total blackness. The next, they were staring at a wall of wavering light. It brightened with each step they took. Inside the ward, a pair of white ravens perched on a Sitka limb. Lush, shoulder-high ferns filled the spaces between the trees.

Ashley's lungs struggled to draw in air. "We're there. Let's keep going. Maybe, we'll find Jane and Crystal."

She ran forward, then hit a flexible barrier and bounced back, falling on her butt. "Bloody hell, what's this now? That freaking hurt."

Behind them, Lennon heard a dog baying. The vibration of heavy boots rushed towards them.

"The ward has been raised again. We're on the wrong side."

CHAPTER 33

ASHLEY WAS SO COLD, HER vital organs were
fusing to her bones. Not to mention she was thirsty
and starving. And, enemies were everywhere. She'd
lost count of the evil guys after them. She didn't
know if her friends were still alive. She couldn't
run another step. She sat down on the frosty, crusty
ground and stared into the tropical rainforest where
the sun always shone and, more importantly, it was
warm.

She had no strength left to fight, especially
when it was futile. She pressed her body against
the undulating wall that might just as well have
been made of brick. But, warmth from the barrier
comforted her a little. She closed her eyes and waited
to be captured or killed.

She raised her eyelids when Lennon dropped

down beside her. He put an arm around her and she huddled closer to him.

With one hand, he pushed at the mystical barrier. His fingers stretched it, then it repelled him and he drew back his hand. "That tingles."

"Well, I hit it full-body. I know it tingles."

She tried to block out the fate approaching them through the gloomy forest. Growling dog and pounding footsteps. The enemy would be upon them in seconds.

She pressed Lennon's hand to her face. "I'm sorry I've been so mean to you. I should have been a better friend."

Lennon tightened the arm holding her. "And, I'm sorry I couldn't protect you."

"It's my job to protect *you*."

"What? That's not how it works ..." He jerked away and leaped up, dragging her with him. He turned her to face the warded forest.

So close they could touch them if it wasn't for the impenetrable barricade, stood a line of four black-robed, hooded figures.

Ashley sucked in a breath, then couldn't let it out. Each figure wore a white mask with the features inked in black. Every mask was an animal emoji, drawn with varying degrees of skill. The emojis were as scary as hell. Like clowns. Ashley never liked clowns, refusing to have one at any of her childhood birthday parties.

She forced the air from her lungs. "I'm done. Just kill me fast." She sank to her knees. The last images in her life would be Frog Face, Sun Face, Fox Face, and Mouse Face.

Behind her, she imagined the hot breath on her neck from the tracker dog. Would tranquilizer darts or bullets be next? Ahead, monsters from an alien world waited. No place to go, no way out.

What the rockin' hell was this? Sun Face beckoned with a curled, pointy finger, like, come with us, we'll save you. Yeah, right.

In a final gesture of defiance, Ashley held up a clenched fist to the line of robed figures, then jabbed at the barrier with her elbow. Like, if I could only get at you, we'd have a throw down, losers.

A riot of sounds burst over the forest behind them. Before she even turned around, Ashley knew it was over. The unleashed dog surged into view. The soldiers would be steps behind.

Sun Face reached through the ward and pulled Ashley in. Frog Face grabbed Lennon by the collar and yanked him through. The rippling wall closed behind them.

One threat at a time. Ashley detached herself from the grasp of Sun Face who, now that Ashley was this close, turned out to be shorter than her. She might be able to take this one, but she and Lennon couldn't take down all four.

Moving closer to the barrier, Ashley flung up her

middle finger at the soldiers as they surged from the winter forest. It was a wasted gesture. The soldiers appeared confused, walking in circles and examining the ground. The dog followed the humans, tail dragging, its tongue hanging.

A female voice spoke into her ear. "They can't hear or see you, Ashley."

Startled, Ashley took a quick step back from Sun Face. "We saw you. Why can't they?"

"Only those who are capable of wielding magic can see or enter the warded area of the forest. Unless we allow it. I wanted you to enter on your own, to realize you can do it, but we ran out of time. The ward was weakened when you entered the forest beside the train tracks yesterday morning. You may have noticed the slight resistance. I'm afraid that's how the young Saskie got out a few weeks ago."

Ashley couldn't be more confused if a dinosaur had waved at her from behind a tree. But, it wasn't dinosaurs that stepped from behind the old growth trees. She counted six additional robed figures, cowls pulled up around their emoji-masked faces. Ten in all. She and Lennon were totally captured. Again.

Show no fear. That should be a good start. "Why are you all masked?" Beside her, Lennon nudged her but she shook him off.

"If possible, we don't want our identities outed," the woman replied, like that was a rational reason to run around a forest with their faces covered in home-made masks, flinging magic around to confuse innocent teenagers.

"But, come." The woman took Ashley and Lennon by their hands. "You must be hungry and dehydrated. When you feel better, we'll see about getting you home. School tomorrow."

CHAPTER 34

LENNON DECIDED HE WAS IN a coma and dreaming this. Or dead and he'd landed in some horrific afterlife. He didn't like either option. Even his room at the abandoned hospital would be welcomed after this. Not that he believed these witches or sorcerers would let them go. They knew Hank was a Sasquatch.

Ashley pulled her hand free. "We have to find our friends. Have you seen them?"

"We're here, Ash." Jane stepped away from a majestic Douglas fir with Crystal right behind her. They looked grubby and bruised but unafraid and, more importantly, well-fed.

Lennon stood aside as Ashley launched herself at her two best friends. Squealing and dramatic arm gestures followed. He sensed that some of the robed dudes were rolling their eyes behind their masks. Taking a closer look at the forms under the black cloaks, Lennon realized Sun Face wasn't the only woman.

He was nearly knocked off his feet as Crystal and Jane threw themselves on him.

"We were so worried about you." Crystal patted his arm, her unbound hair flapping in his face. Both she and Jane looked like they had spent years in the wild instead of less than two days. Two days? It had to be longer than that judging by the way his stomach roiled with hunger.

Jane thumped his shoulder over and over. "Epic glad you're okay. Thought they got you."

"They did. We got away. So, the ninjas just left you and Crystal on the ground under the tree?" He didn't want to mention it to Ashley earlier, but he was sure her best friends had been killed by the ninjas.

Sun Face answered. "The Omega fighters knew we were trying to raise the ward again which would trap them inside with us. That's likely why they didn't take the time to kill Jane and Crystal. They counted on the girls dying in the forest. We found them still unconscious."

Despite having no clue about what was going on, Lennon's body began to relax for the first time in ... forever, it seemed. Mentally, he was still on his guard with these Halloween-garbed people. Friend or foe? Did they want something from him? If so, he hadn't a clue what. If anyone here had nothing of value, it was him.

Outside the protective shield, the dog and six heavily-armed soldiers wandered aimlessly. Sun Face saw his glance and said, "They'll find their way back to their helicopter eventually. Proximity to the ward disorients regular folk for a while. From above, this portion of the forest looks like any other. Except, if they try to land here, they'll find themselves — well, somewhere else. You can call me Prin."

Prin? As in Princess? Lennon and the girls followed Prin deeper into the forest of perpetual high-noon summer where they weren't affected by the freezing temperatures outside. It was good to feel the swish of moist ferns against his shoulders and enjoy the mingled fragrance of the pines and spruce. The lone spectre of a long-dead trapper crossed their path. Did Prin's head turn briefly in its direction? The spectre glided around some giant trees; the smaller ones it walked *through*. Guess those had sprung up since he died. At least this "energy remnant" didn't try to give him directions.

They watched in awe as one of the robed gang started a campfire using small branches from fallen trees and a bolt of flame that shot out of his hand. Lennon could do that too. Or, he could make things smoke. He hadn't told anyone, though.

Four hot dogs and a litre of chocolate milk later,

Lennon decided he wasn't going to join the spectre realm today. Tonight? Now, he wanted to lay down on the damp ground and sleep for a week. Beside him, Ashley's body slumped against a tree as she fought to stay awake while Crystal and Jane chattered at her.

From the corner of his eye, he watched Prin and two other people — a man and a woman, Fox Face and Mouse Face — in close discussion. From the rigid way they held their bodies, Lennon guessed something serious was up. Dozens of ravens peered down at them, small white blobs against the green fir needles. The black-spotted raven fixed its glittery eyes on Lennon and ignored its branch mates.

Prin sat down with them and folded her hands together. They weren't wrinkly or spotted from the sun. Since her hands were the only body parts Lennon had to go by, he judged her age to be around thirty or forty. The man and woman, Fox Face and Mouse Face, dropped to the ground beside Prin.

"Change of plan," Prin began. "I need to give you the quick and dirty explanation since it looks like we don't have as much time as I'd hoped."

Jane nudged Ashley into wakefulness and the three girls sat rigidly upright, probably wondering what was going to hit them now. Lennon took a last gulp of chocolate milk and readied himself for more bad news.

Prin paused as though trying to find the right words, or the right place to start, filtering out unnecessary details.

She gestured at her companions. "Fox and Mouse just returned from patrolling the outer boundaries of the sanctuary. There are 11 bodies at the bottom of the meteorite impact crater. The loggers appear to have been thrown off the cliff by the four Omega fighters who pursued you through the forest and captured Lennon and Ashley."

"That's why the loggers stopped chasing us," Ashley exclaimed, all signs of fatigue absent now. "I figured they just ran out of bullets and gave up."

Prin nodded. "The loggers may have given up eventually, but Omega fighters never surrender, not until they themselves are captured or die."

"The rat bastards shook us out of the tree and knocked us out," Crystal contributed. Her expression promised vengeance if she ever came across those men again.

Remembering how she had jumped back into battle with the crazed, infected bikers a few months ago when all seemed lost, Lennon would bet on her, hands down.

"Who is Omega?" Lennon had so many questions, he didn't know where to start, and Prin had mentioned Omega a couple of times. It had to be important.

"Omega is a multi-national corporation with many business interests. Supplying arms and personnel to both sides of various wars is one of the more distasteful. A very dangerous project they are currently pursuing is the use of telepathy in warfare. They know that the Keepers — that's us — use telepathy, and they would do anything to capture us."

"But, why do they want Lennon and Ashley?" Jane asked.

"I'm guessing they know your history with the infected biker gang. As do we." Prin turned her masked face from one to another of the teens. "You may not realize it yet, but you four exhibit signs of latent magical ability or you wouldn't have been able to defeat the bikers. Which means you are Keepers, too, or will be if you decide to join us someday."

"What exactly is it you do? What do you 'keep'?" Lennon didn't have a freaking clue what was happening here, but he wasn't about to join a shadow group even if they had saved their lives.

"We consider ourselves librarians and curators. We gather and store knowledge and artifacts to preserve history, so our descendants don't make the same mistakes humans have made in the past."

Lennon exchanged glances with Ashley. They didn't have to use thought transference to be on the same page here. These people were not 100 percent playing with a full deck.

Prin continued as though she hadn't noticed the exchange between the two. "Climate change occurs cyclically on this planet. We're in the throes of another cycle and it's happening more quickly than in the past, due mostly to humankind's stupidity, but I won't go into all that. Look it up if you don't already know.

"There will be world-wide temperature rises, warming and acidification of oceans, rising sea levels, decreased snow cover. All this will result in massive flooding, monster storms — the list goes on and on, including possible separation of continents, even a polar shift."

Lennon knew all this. They studied global warming, but they could possibly reverse things if greedy mega-corporations got on board. Didn't sound like that was likely, though.

"Many, if not most, animal species will become extinct. The rest will eventually evolve to adapt to new conditions. Humans are also at great risk of mass annihilation, especially those living near coastlines. It's happened before, and each time, we've had to crawl out of the rubble and start all over."

In his peripheral vision, Lennon glimpsed the greenish glow of a spectre plodding through the forest. Whether a trapper, First Nations, or a modern-day hiker, he didn't turn to find out. Prin was making this whole global warming thing sound imminent and scary as hell, and energy remnants seemed kind of unimportant and ordinary.

CHAPTER 35

ASHLEY WAS WIDE AWAKE NOW. She didn't want to crawl out of any rubble. What about cell towers and internet?

With a glance behind her at the ward, Prin continued, "For thousands of years, our group has existed to ensure that, after planetary chaos, we don't forget the past. We want to make sure survivors have stepping stones to rebuild. We have Keeper Packets all over the world, each working independently to gather information from our specific geographical locations, and to prevent global infiltration from our enemies. In this era, one of the greater threats is Omega Incorporated. They don't care about preservation or the future of the planet. They are focussed on war and the money to be made by creating more destructive weapons. Including harnessing the power of the mind."

Crystal raised her arm like she was in class. "Um, what's a packet and does your group have a special name?"

Jane rolled her eyes, twice, and gave Crystal a shove.

"A Packet is what we call a specific Keeper group. There are four in Canada, dozens around the world. The word 'packet' sounds less threatening than 'cell' and is less likely to set off alarms if anyone overhears members talking, which should never happen."

Ashley had a glimmer of understanding. "What name did the Keepers go by in the past, if you don't mind me asking?"

Prin nodded at her approvingly. "There were many. Some you might recognize include Druid, Knights Templar, Rosicrucian, Illuminati — the list is a long one dating back through the millennia. Most of these societies are known historically for other reasons, but all held to one abiding principle – preservation of the human race in the face of world catastrophe. Initially, we were a self-effacing bunch, doing our best to avoid the attention of the authorities. After the Romans slaughtered most of the Druids, we had to learn to fight. We have a mission statement that has endured for many thousands of years — Life Everlasting."

She looked at an old-fashioned watch — well, what else would work in this dead zone? "Since Confederation in 1867, this country has introduced its own Keeper Packets." Prin indicated the other robed figures. "We are the western Packet with never more than 25 members, deliberately kept to a low membership since we don't use modern technology to communicate. In the north-central area of the country, under the guise of mining, we have built a colossal series of tunnels and underground archives, including living areas to sustain life for years until the planet's surface is stable. We are moving the Saskie clan to a new sanctuary close to one of the entrances to the tunnels."

Ashley couldn't process the torrent of information. She fixed on one fact. "There are only 10 Keepers here. You said there are 25 in your Packet."

"We use inter-consciousness means of transferring messages and information, or telepathy if you will. This is the reason we limit our membership to those warriors who demonstrate magical abilities. Mind connection seems to be a natural talent among mystical beings, but there's a limit to how many minds can be connected without energetic weakness occurring. And, yes, we're aren't all present. One of our number is a surgeon and unavailable; two police officers are on duty; and a few others are out of the country. We've never had our full number present during an operation. When we realized the ward was failing, I called in as many as possible, and we managed to strengthen it as soon as the protected area was clear of interlopers. The four Keepers who were inside the sanctuary at the time you entered tried to keep you in sight. But, they had illegal loggers to contend with as well as the Omega fighters."

"How did you get to be magical beings?" Crystal interrupted.

"Good question. It seems to be mostly a crap-shoot as far as DNA goes. Thankfully, researchers haven't isolated the genetic code for magic yet, and believe me, it's not for lack of trying. More about that later. Most of us don't know we have any special abilities until something triggers them — usually a trauma to our brain, either physical or psychological."

A shiver ran through Ashley's body. "Like, maybe a plague virus like LM43?"

"Long story. And, not the one you've been told. Frog has gone to check on the whereabouts of the mercenaries. It's just a matter of time until they figure out something unnatural is going on and call in reinforcements. They can surround the ward and wait us out. We have to leave immediately and move the Saskies to their new sanctuary. Once everyone is loaded into the trucks, we'll lower the ward and return these 12 acres to their natural state. I'll explain more on the way back to Victoria."

"Wait!" Ashley blurted. "You just said '12 acres'. We were in here for hours, maybe days, running all over, trying to find our way back to the train tracks."

"And, what's the ward for, anyway?" Crystal asked. "We've only seen ravens and Saskies."

Prin reached under her mask to scratch her chin. "One of the side effects of raising a ward is time, space, and temperature distortion within the protection area. We created a sanctuary, and 12 acres was enough to sustain the last colony of *Homo sasqua* in North America. They thrive within a wide temperature range. We moved other species out because they didn't seem to be comfortable here. The white ravens are an exception. They are able to fly in and out as they wish."

"What's a Homo sasqua thingie?" Jane's expression made it clear she was on information overload, or maybe it was just her flattened hair that caused her to look 14 instead of 16.

"Our Saskies. Their DNA is closer to human than even the chimpanzee and the bonobo." From low in her throat, Prin made a loud *chk-chk-chk* sound.

Ashely heard the trees rustling, like a breeze had finally found its way through this strange forest. Long fingers parted the needles of a pine tree and round, golden eyes rimmed in black flickered in apprehension.

After another *chk-chk-chk* from Prin, dozens of thick, furry bodies clambered down the trunks of nearby trees, or dropped from lower limbs.

A smaller Sasquatch wearing a brown jacket and checked trapper hat hurled itself at Lennon, knocking him over.

"Hank!" Lennon threw his arms around the neck of his friend.

"Even considering the heat in here, we can't get

the coat and hat off that one," Prin explained. "No need to worry by the way — they're herbivorous."

CHAPTER 36

GRUNTING EXCITEDLY, HANK PICKED UP
Lennon and carried him over to a couple of larger
Sasquatches standing together. Their fur was
slightly darker than Hank's golden-brown, but still
lighter than several of the others. Soon, Hank and
his parents were thumping Lennon on the back
and snuffling at his hair and neck. Jane and Crystal
squealed and ran over to the group to hug Hank.
They received the same sniff test from his parents.

From the corner of his eye, Lennon noticed
Ashley hovering nearby. "It's Hank," he called to
her. Good thing she didn't have her dagger, or there
might be a throw down with the Sasquatches. She
wasn't getting what a unique experience it was to
witness these creatures that everyone thought were
mythical.

Jane and Crystal left Hank's family and petted and fussed over a baby in the arms of its mother, the proud father sniffing at the girls' necks. The fur on this family unit was more yellow than brown, with the baby almost white-blond.

Prin waited while the Sasquatches sniffed and touched the new humans, then she *chk-chk-chked* again. The Sasquatches gathered around while Prin conversed with them in a language that consisted of mainly consonants with a few cat-like sounds thrown in. Most of them had questions. They didn't seem to be taking the news of their move to their new northern home well, and there were a few side conversations taking place among the adult Sasquatches. Crystal and Jane entertained the kids with a game of hide and seek among the ferns. The kids imitated the girls' giggles and Lennon kind of hoped the little ones wouldn't forget their last night in this protected paradise.

Ashley stood alone, back against a trunk, almost hidden behind the fronds of chest-high ferns. Lennon could tell by the way her hands clenched and unclenched, that she didn't trust anything about this situation. Why was she always on alert, unable to relax and enjoy the moment? This experience was as mind blowing as finding out dragons were real.

Two dark brown elders managed to get the rest of the colony resting quietly, waiting for transport to their new home, likely many days' travel away.

Lennon tightened his arm around Hank's shoulder. After he and the girls were dropped off in Victoria, he would never see Hank again, but maybe Prin would let him know when Hank and the others were safe.

A blooping sound from the direction of the protective barrier preceded the arrival of Frog Face, a white raven riding on his shoulder. Lennon turned up the volume on his hearing.

Frog Face walked close to Prin and touched her shoulder briefly before turning to look at the teens. "Evening, lad and ladies. I'm Frog, Prin's Protector."

Before Lennon had a chance to ask what a Protector was, Frog addressed Prin. "Another chopper has left the mainland, headed for the Island. Our white-feathered friend here reports the men from the first chopper plus the Omega fighters who kidnapped the kids are staying close to the logging camp for now." This was the first time Lennon had heard any of the Keepers speak out loud other than Prin, and he tried to memorize the voice in case he heard it again. Frog had a British accent which might help identify him. He seemed to be Prin's second in command.

Prin called to her followers, "Start in the centre and work your way to the perimeter, notifying each tree that we are lowering the ward. They've been used to a tropical climate for the past 15 years, and they'll need to prepare their roots for the change in temperature. That's everyone except Cat, Fox, and

Mouse who will load the Saskies into the trucks. At the airport, our transport plane is waiting to take us to a destination I'll share with you in-flight. Travel information from there will be kept secret until the next leg of the journey. Anyone who can't be away from home or job for the next week, speak to me telepathically in the truck on the way to Victoria."

Lennon had a dozen questions he wanted to ask Prin but realized this wasn't the time. Maybe, he could contact her mind once they were on the move. What would happen if she was connected to someone else's mind when he tried contacting her? Would he get some kind of busy signal, or a piercing head pain?

Jane and Crystal came up carrying four backpacks and armfuls of weapons. Ashley grabbed her dagger and slammed it into her back holster. Lennon accepted his curved knife and placed it into his backpack, careful not to slice his new winter jacket.

Fox and Cat began herding the Saskies together and leading them into the forest. Shouldn't he and the girls be following, too?

Mouse turned her mask toward Prin. "What about these kids? We have three trucks. Where are we supposed to put them? We've already got the 10 of us, 38 Saskies, and supplies including a weeks' worth of food."

'We're only taking them as far as the airport," Prin replied. "If we have to, we'll strap them to the roof of a truck."

CHAPTER 37

"FIRST, THOUGH," PRIN POINTED AT the four teens. "You are going to help us lower the ward. It will be good practice for you."

Ashley remembered the strange thing Lennon had done when she and her friends jumped into the meteorite lake. He'd saved them from falling to their deaths by pulling them away from the cliff face and directing them into the middle of the lake. Then there was the super speed and enhanced senses he retained even after he received the vaccine against LM43. From what Prin said earlier, he wasn't the only one left with peculiar side effects.

"Lennon has magical abilities," she confided to Prin. "The rest of us don't." Ashley didn't mention the telepathy thing between her and Lennon.

Jane and Crystal looked uneasy, like they were

going to take a test they hadn't prepared for. Failure wasn't just an option here, it was inevitable.

"We shall soon see," Prin responded cheerfully. She led them through the forest, back to the shield that protected the Saskies and old growth trees from predatory humans. The dark, wintry side was free from mercenaries, dogs, or Omega fighters.

Prin held her hand close to the rippling wall. "Touch the barrier. Tell me what you feel."

Without hesitation, Jane swept her hand back and forth. Crystal did the same but more tentatively.

"Tingly," Jane said.

"Same." Crystal looked at her hand and seemed surprised she still had fingers.

Ashley was tempted to roll her eyes, but put her hand out. "It's an energy field, I guess."

Lennon just stood there like he was too cool to take part in the exercise. Ashley prodded him in the back. He stayed where he was and said, "I can feel it from back here."

"Very good. Now, do this." Prin thrust her arm through. She watched as Ashley and Jane obediently shoved an arm through the barrier. Lennon stepped forward and followed Prin's instruction.

Crystal pushed both arms through and stated, "Totally amazing. So, does this mean we can do other stuff, too?"

"It certainly does. Right now, I want you all to connect with the energy of the ward. Your magic wants to do it; you simply have to allow it. That takes practice. The successful lowering of the ward doesn't depend on you, but the experience will open you up to other possibilities."

Prin suddenly turned away and inclined her head. After several long moments, she said, "The Saskies are loaded, and the trees have been notified of the imminent drop in temperature. Keepers are in place around the sanctuary. Now we can lower the ward and go. Helicopters are approaching. We're out of time."

Ashley began to hyperventilate and forced herself to stop taking in rapid breaths. Soldiers and ninja fighters, not to mention Sasquatches were real, and magic existed. Once she got home — *if* she got home — there would be no more weird stuff for her. The others could do whatever, but Ashley wanted no part of magic. Not now, not ever.

"Spread out along the wall. I'll be directing the take-down. If you can, allow me access to your minds and you can follow along with the rest of us. Shut your eyes and stand close to the ward, but don't touch it or you'll be knocked on your asses."

Ashley caught Lennon's eye and he smirked. She looked away and checked there were no humans on the other side. A few white ravens watched curiously. She closed her eyes and concentrated on the ward.

Her eyelids flew open at a gentle tugging sensation in her brain. She glanced at Lennon again, but he shook his head at her. Wasn't him. Ashley closed her eyes and allowed her mind to welcome the tugging. The sensation stopped and she heard words in her mind. Not Lennon's. Prin's.

Everyone ready? Good. We begin. Focus on the ward. Its energy returns to us. We are one.

Ashley didn't really want to do this. She squeezed her eyelids and tried to hang on to her sense of self. The energy of the ward was soft and comforting. She couldn't resist allowing it to bathe her in its warmth. She sensed a light brighter than that of the forest and wanted to open her eyes to see it, but was afraid it might scorch her eyeballs.

Absorb it. The energy of the ward originated with us. Let it return to us.

A soothing, familiar essence mingled with hers until it was all the same. Lennon, and then Crystal and Jane. Prin. All the other Keepers. Even the Saskies and the white ravens. She joined the ferns, the trees. And, the flowers that sprinkled the forest floor. What *was* this?

The energy became almost painful in its intensity. So much power. In a brief flash of understanding, Ashley knew she was connected to every particle in the cosmos.

Then, the connection was severed and Ashley experienced a sense of loss.

It is done. Now, we run to the trucks and leave this place behind.

Ashley didn't want to leave. She wanted to stay

here and be every living thing in the world; to become one with the universal pattern again.

Prin clapped her on the back. "Back to reality, Ashley. You can think about this experience later. We're no longer protected from our enemies."

Ashley opened her eyes. A chill blew in, softly at first, then more rapidly, as though winter had been held at bay too long from this sacred place. Gone was the rainforest humidity. Gone were the shafts of summer sunlight that had pierced the green canopy and divided the forest floor into irregular segments.

Prin shook Lennon, Jane, and Crystal out of their trances. "Everyone, follow me." She pointed up at a half dozen white ravens, barely visible in the branches. "Lead."

The Keeper sprinted after the ravens, and Ashley soon lost them in the encroaching darkness. Lennon grabbed her hand. "Hang onto the others. I can keep Prin in sight."

"Jane, take Crystal's hand and don't let go." Once Ashley was sure they were linked, she said to Lennon, "Let's go home."

CHAPTER 38

THE RAVENS GLIDED THROUGH THE forest, Prin running behind. Lennon was able to keep them in sight, barely. Prin was fast, but he could have been out in front if he didn't have to moderate his speed to accommodate the girls. Just as well since he didn't know where he was going.

Lennon figured they would be running for miles and worried that the girls wouldn't be up for another long dash through the forest — well, he wasn't as concerned for Ashley. He knew from their battles with the bikers and ninjas that she was tough and nothing seemed to stop her for long. It must be due to the magic that Prin said they all possessed.

By the time they erupted from the forest. Lennon had lost all sense of direction and wouldn't have been surprised if they had arrived at the railway tracks. Nope.

This was an uneven, dirt road, probably an abandoned logging road. Three rusting canopied military troop carriers waited. The motors were running, rasping like they were taking their last breaths. The winter chill raised goosebumps on his bare arms.

Frog and Fox waited by the back of the last truck. Prin stepped onto the back fender and vaulted over the tailgate unaided. Lennon stood to one side to allow the girls to board but two Keepers lifted him by the armpits and threw him in. He got to his hands and knees a fraction of a second before Ashley landed next to him, swearing loudly. Crystal, Jane, and four backpacks joined the heap in the middle of the truck bed.

Long benches ran along each length of the interior, with at least a half dozen Saskies sitting on each, several babies and toddlers perched on their laps. White ravens clung to furry shoulders, a few opting for the view from the tops of heads. Frog and Fox remained standing outside on the fender. They drew a piece of canvas across the back, leaving the passengers in darkness. The idling truck ground into gear and rumbled forward.

Prin's and Mouse's white masks and the ravens were faint points of light, unless you counted the round, yellow Saskie eyes blinking at random. The fur-covered arm that reached out and pulled Lennon out of the pile of girls turned out to belong to Hank, seated beside his family.

Lennon had shown Hank how to fist-bump, and now he didn't care how dumb it looked, he bumped

Hank, twice. One of the girls got out a tiny, jewelled flashlight and used the light to find seats, hip-checking the Saskies until they moved over.

A few more hours and they would be home. He would miss Hank a lot, but he was too tired to think about that right now. If only he could skip school tomorrow. Except, he didn't have anyone to write him a note, and he had no way of contacting Mrs. Wilson to ask her to cover for him when the school called about his absence.

The black-splotched raven hopped over to squat on Lennon's shoulder, laying its beak alongside his cheek as though to comfort him. Lennon wanted to brush the bird away but didn't have the nerve — that was one sharp beak. No raven could take Hank's place. No point in it trying.

CHAPTER 39

IT WAS TIGHT IN THE confines of the truck bed. At least Ashley had an end seat next to the flapping tarp where she didn't feel too claustrophobic yet. The air quality was disgusting, though.

She pushed aside the tarp and said to Fox who was hanging onto a hand rail, "Can we have this flap open? It smells worse than a chicken coop in here." Not that she'd ever been in a chicken coop, but she'd heard stories.

"Sorry, love," the other one — Frog, the Protector — replied. "We want to keep you warm and snug in there." His British accent was actually kind of sexy, but Ashley was in no state to appreciate it.

She snorted. "I may puke."

Both Keepers laughed. Frog said, "Give us a warning if you decide on that route, will you, love? I'll jump out of the way."

Ashley yanked the canvas back in place. Rude, much? Between the smell and the jolting of the vehicle, she wasn't kidding about the barfing. This antique army truck hit a pothole every few metres. And, she was sure she recognized the laugh from Fox, the one that didn't speak.

Jane's voice reached Ashley from somewhere near the far end of her bench. "I think some of this smell is us."

Ashley heard a loud sniff, then Jane said, "Yup, I'm really ripe. And these cute little Saskies aren't wearing diapers. I'm covered in Sasquatch pee. Other stuff, too."

Lennon was the next to complain. "This raven just pooped down the back of my shirt. Why are the birds riding inside with us? They can fly. I thought they were staying in the forest?"

"I guess they decided to come with us," Prin replied. "It remains to be seen if they get on the plane. Their choice."

"I've lost every single one of my skull beads." Crystal announced. "Every. Single. One. What are my parents going to say when they see me? I look like I've been dragged behind a mule during spring planting."

"You've never seen a mule." Ashley didn't care what they looked like. Her tribulations the past 36 hours far surpassed her friends'. "I was zapped with a tranquilizer and dragged through a forest tied to a stretcher and almost ..."

'We were tranquilized, too ..." Jane began.

"Alright!" Prin's white Sun mask floated in the darkness. By her tone, she'd had enough complaints.

Ashley jumped. She had almost forgotten Prin was sitting across from her.

"You'll soon be home. Clean, warm, and safe. Please remember that our Saskies have a long and dangerous journey ahead of them. Keep in mind, they are closer to human than any other creature on the planet. They only lack the ability to feel aggression without provocation. Some might say they are more evolved than us — and I'd be one of them."

"Sorry," Ashley mumbled.

The others echoed the apology, but Ashley heard Crystal add, "I'm especially sorry I didn't go home after training Friday night and stay there."

Jane groaned. "Every bone in my body hurts. I've been wondering why the ninja creeps didn't take the Saskie that fell out of the tree with us. You'd think he'd be a real prize for an evil corporation like Omega."

Prin's brisk tone answered her. "Saskies are fast when they're in danger. He — or she — must have run off before the Omega warriors could react."

Ashley's entire right side was a sweaty mess where she was crushed against a male Saskie who wouldn't quit smelling her hair. She had lost her ponytail elastic during the nightmare journey through the tunnel, and her hair fell around her face in limp strands. Who knew what lurked inside the filthy tangle. Whatever, the Saskie obviously thought it was delicious. The truck hit another pothole and the Saskie took the opportunity to slide closer. Ashley prodded him in the stomach with her elbow and he edged away, but not far enough. God, would this horror never end?

"How about I tell you more about us?" Prin's mask swivelled slowly from side to side. "I've told you about the Keepers and our mission — to prevent intelligent life on this planet from disappearing in the chaos of climate change. I've asked you to consider joining us, after you complete your educations in whatever fields you are passionate about. All four of you have magical abilities. Lennon's magic is the strongest. The so-called LM43 virus was the trigger."

Ashley had stuck her head out the back for another breath of actual breathable air before she added three second-hand hot dogs to the mess on the floor. Frog and Fox conversed quietly. As soon as her head emerged through the flap, they stopped talking. But, she had already noticed something about the second Keeper, Fox, not Frog who called her "love". The mask muffled his words, but there was something familiar about the timbre of Fox's voice. She knew him. If only she could figure out from where.

CHAPTER 40

LENNON SAID, "PRIN, DO YOU mean that everyone who got the virus has super powers now, or magical abilities? Fifteen thousand people on Vancouver Island were infected."

"Yeah, because you said Ashley and Jane and I can do magic, but we never got bit by someone with the virus." Crystal added.

"I'm saying that the virus was an extreme stressor on the general population. In a few, it triggered latent paranormal abilities. There aren't too many things more stressful than having family members and classmates succumb to what a lot of people thought were vampires. As it happened, only a dozen people who were bitten, all of them under the age of eighteen, have displayed paranormal tendencies. We know who the others are and are monitoring them, as we monitored you four."

"Why?" Ashley asked, bewildered. "Why watch us? And, who?"

"Keeper Packets have eyes in the police, in schools, hospitals, government departments, pretty much everywhere. And, we can communicate instantaneously. Better than texting. And, just for the record, the only individuals with enhanced strength, speed, hearing, eyesight, and healing are those with latent paranormal abilities who were bitten and fell victim to the virus, with accompanying fangs and blood-thirst."

"Gee-zuz," Ashley said, "I am totally confused. You say all four of us are paranormals, but for different reasons?"

Prin didn't answer for a while. Lennon suspected she was listening to a voice in her head. Probably more crap was coming their way.

"Okay, let me put it this way. All of you had the capability for magic which lay dormant. About 10 per cent of the population are born with the genetic coding that makes magic possible. Lennon was infected by a member of the outlaw biker gang and obtained not only a fine set of fangs, but all the accompanying enhancements. After the vaccine was administered, Lennon retained these abilities due to his magic gene triggered by the stress.

"The bikers have reverted to their former nasty, evil, human forms without powers. Even if they were born with the genetic marker — which has not yet been identified by mainstream science, as I've mentioned before — they were physically mature and as mentally mature as they were ever going to be. So, that takes care of the difference between Lennon and the bikers. Got that part?"

Over the rumbling of the truck's engine, the Saskies conversed in their guttural language, paying no attention to Prin's explanation. Even with a chatty Saskie seated between him and Prin, Lennon had no problem hearing her. His concern was for the girls. He didn't want to have to explain this all to them later, especially since he wasn't sure he understood it himself.

"Can I just recap what you've said so far, Prin?" Ashley asked.

"By all means." Prin sounded resigned. She didn't know Ashley very well if she thought this was going to go smoothly.

"Okay, so somehow the bikers caught this strange virus. They bit a lot of people, infecting them, including Lennon. After the cure, the bikers lost their super powers because they were old and non-magical. Lennon is young and was magical all along, so now he's not only able to perform magic, but he's still got his powers from the virus. That about it?"

"Good summary, Ashley," Prin responded. "I wish I'd said that. Did you mention you want to be a lawyer? Next, I'll explain how you three girls are involved in our little circle of extra-normal beings."

"Oh, good," Crystal commented. The baby Saskie on her lap squealed with delight as Crystal bounced up and down on the wood seat.

"Chill, Crystal," Ashley warned. "You'll make that baby pee again."

"Mine's asleep," Jane announced. "She's so cute. I wish I could keep her."

"Well you can't." Lennon needed to set her straight. "They eat a ton of vegetables every day, and it's worse than cleaning up after a horse. Besides, she'd miss her family."

Prin asked, "Do you want to hear more or not?"

"Hell, yeah," Jane told her. "Ignore Lennon. He's always interrupting."

"Now, you three girls have probably been friends for a very long time, right?" Prin didn't wait for an answer, probably knew she'd be sorry she asked the question. "From what I've seen, you're all very different. There's a reason you gravitated towards each other which I won't go into now since it's rather metaphysical, and I don't really understand it myself. Anyway, you were mean to Lennon in school, tormenting him and making his life more miserable than it needed to be — oh, yes you did, don't bother to make excuses."

She overrode the indignant denials of the three girls. A twinge of satisfaction at the validation washed over Lennon. They had been mean before the plague. During the plague, they were meaner.

"You thought he was a vampire. But, you didn't kill him when you had the chance. And, he didn't kill you, or anyone else, although he was ordered to by his biker masters. The reason for all the non-killing is also above my pay grade. You fought together in a way far superior to your training and any normal ability. I've seen it myself these past few days."

"We're deadly good, for sure," Crystal bragged. "And me with just a *dumb* hammer."

"Don't forget your mini-switchblade, Crys," Jane added.

Prin raised her voice. "You four are what we call a Quartel, a natural group consisting of one Leader, one Protector, and two Guardians. Any guesses who is who?"

"Sure." Crystal stopped bouncing the Saskie baby. "Easy. Ash is the leader, Lennon is her protector, which leaves Jane and me as the guardians."

"Close but wrong," Prin said. "You are warriors, like all Keepers. Crystal and Jane are Guardians, but Lennon is the Leader and Ashley is the Protector. In case you haven't figured it out, my name is short for *princeps* which is Latin for leader. Frog is my Protector, while Fox and Mouse are my Guardians. We form a Quartel. One day, after we have fallen in battle or retired, the shield will pass to your generation and you will continue the mission."

The sound of human voices ceased at Prin's

pronouncement, leaving only the Saskie and raven conversations underlying the mechanical noises of the truck engine and the rhythmical slapping of helicopter blades in the distance. Lennon wanted to be wrong about the chopper but knew he wasn't.

He waited for Ashley to pitch a fit. Prin had to be wrong. Ashley was always jumping in front of him, wanting to go first, arguing about whose plan was better, poking him with her finger. If bossy was a leadership quality, then Ashley was the heir, not him.

Ashley's calm voice surprised him. "I guess that's why I always know where Lennon is, and why I feel protective. Uberbummer."

Then, she added, "I don't see any place in the Keeper world for a lawyer, so I guess you'll have to find another Protector for Lennon."

"But, Ash," Jane's voice cracked, "we're a team, a *Quartel*!"

Prin cleared her throat to regain their attention. "The driver of this truck? She's a lawyer. Crown Attorney, to be specific."

Then, Ashley sensed Prin go still. She remained quiet for so long, the Saskies stopped jabbering and listened as intently as Lennon and the girls.

Prin's white mask disappeared. Lennon caught a fleeting glimpse of blurred features before she pulled a black ski mask over her face in its place. She cast the long cloak aside to reveal a black outfit of tight-fitting shirt and pants. Reaching underneath her seat, she produced an assault rifle, then rummaged for something else. Lennon flinched as a magazine slammed into place.

Finally, Prin spoke. "Sentries report two choppers on our tail. There's a break in the forest up ahead. We'll pull in there. Be ready to fight."

CHAPTER 41

ASHLEY CLUNG TO THE WOODEN seat with her fingers. The trucks sped into the forest until the lead vehicle bumped up against the massive trunk of a Douglas fir. The driver of the third truck was forced to stop with the front bumper touching the back of the second. The truck's back end projected several feet onto the rutted logging road.

She picked up her backpack from near her feet and exited the truck amid a flurry of Saskies, ravens, and humans. She didn't care what the others decided. She didn't want any part of this Keeper business. This was it for her, whether she survived or not. Hadn't she already decided this? Shit just kept on happening, though.

The Saskies snatched up their children and took to the trees. Nearby branches shook violently, then stilled. The white ravens flew into the forest and disappeared from view. Like Prin's, the other Keepers' faces were concealed with black ski masks. Body-hugging black clothing replaced the cloaks. Each carried a rifle and a leather bag slung over their shoulders. Ashley could only hope the bags contained lots of extra ammo.

"Come with me," Prin ordered.

Ashley found herself part of another hand-holding chain, with Lennon in front, and Jane at the end.

"Can't you just put up a ward again?" she called to Prin.

"We'll try, but it takes more time and focus to raise a ward than it does to lower it. Now, no more talking." Ahead of her, a Keeper lighted Prin's way with a dim flashlight.

How many desperate runs through the forest did this make? It was winter again and none of them had on their warm coats. A sweat-soaked tee shirt didn't cut it. As soon as they stopped, she was going to pull out her jacket, toque, and mitts.

"We make our stand here," Prin announced. She went into one of her listening trances. Glancing around, Ashley didn't see any of the other nine Keepers, but she knew they were close by, invisible and silent.

Ashley's eyes had adjusted to the darkness as much as they were going to. She might as well be blind. She, Crystal, and Jane would have to rely on Lennon's super-duper eyesight.

"Get your coat on, Ash," Jane whispered to her. "It's freaking polar out here."

Ashley struggled into her down-filled jacket, positioning her back holster on the outside within easy reach. She stretched her shoulders to ensure she could get at the weapon in an instant.

Prin said in a low voice, "The mercenaries are ten minutes away. There are a dozen of them with one flame thrower. No sign of the dog or the Omega ninjas but that just means we don't know where they are yet. We have no time to raise a ward."

Facing two crazy, fanged outlaw bikers who didn't bother to use their guns until the last minute was totally different than this gig, with trained fighters armed up the wazoo.

A wave of grief washed over Ashley as she realized she might never see her mom again. Ashley was sorry for giving her such a hard time lately. She knew her parents weren't getting back together, ever, but she couldn't help hating Mom's new boyfriend, no matter how nice he tried to be.

Lennon squeezed her arm and shook her. "Ashley. Come on. Prin said to get as far away from the Keepers as possible. Bring the others."

Ashley prepared herself for another endless race through the forest in complete blackness. Her exhausted brain told her it was Sunday after sunset, but that was a guess. Right now, she had to trust Lennon wouldn't run them into a trunk massive enough to splat all three girls at the same time. She was so done with this shit.

They hadn't run far when Lennon stopped. "We'll take cover behind this fallen trunk and wait to see if we can help."

Was he nuts? "Help with what? The bleeding and dying?"

"Shoot me now," Crystal pleaded. "I can't do this anymore. I think I'm in shock."

"Just move it. You'll be in more than shock if those baddies catch us," Jane replied. "You and I will be dead. Lennon and Ashley will be taken away to some evil lab on the other side of the world."

Ashley stayed silent until they slid over the top of the fallen tree. "We can't stay here. We have to keep moving." Far, far away.

Lennon stood solidly, like his feet had grown roots as deep as the trees surrounding them. "We have to help the Keepers if they need us."

"Okay, let's take stock of our resources here," Ashley responded. "We have one dagger, one hatchet, one useless hammer." She tapped Lennon on the arm, "And, one knife. Against soldiers with military-grade weapons. Oh, and a bunch of ninjas thrown in just for fun."

"Don't forget our cute little switchblades, Ash," Jane added.

Ashley ignored Jane and sank to her knees behind the rotted trunk, reaching into the front pocket of her jeans. She might have dropped her switchblade after escaping from the Omega ninjas. Her fingertips touched the cool marble handle of the knife. Still there but fat lot of good it would do in a fight against scary weapons.

"Oh god, oh god," Crystal whimpered.

"Uh oh." Jane's voice came out hoarse, without its usual bravado.

"What?" Ashley whipped her head around. *Well, shit!*

CHAPTER 42

LENNON CLOSED HIS EYES BRIEFLY before scanning the forest. Fifty yards back, the mercenaries surged into a narrow clearing. The faintest of skylight illuminated a mob of armed soldiers wearing full combat gear, helmets, and carrying assault rifles. One of them hefted an object that caused the blood to drain from Lennon's head, leaving him colder than before.

"That's a grenade launcher. I thought Prin said flame thrower." Shit, what difference did it make to their chances of survival?

The soldiers didn't see the Keepers. They spread out, searching. A sudden weakness overcame Lennon. He leaned against the fallen trunk, the rough wood scraping his face. He longed to curl up against the moss-covered bark and sleep forever.

"We're dead," Crystal announced. "I'll never see my parents again. They'll never know what happened to me. I wish I hadn't lied to them so much."

"You're not being extreme this time, Crys," Jane said. "I bet we've already been reported missing, presumed dead. Might as well make it official."

Ashley rounded on her friends. "Knock it off. Since when do we quit? If we go down, we go down fighting. Besides, it's only Sunday night, I think, so no one will be looking for us yet. Probably." Her thoughts were so contradictory, she didn't know what she meant.

"Yeah, but Ash, they got a grenade launcher." Jane sat with her back to the trunk staring into the dark vastness of the forest. "Once they finish off the Keepers, they'll find us. Where's the damn tracker dog anyway? Wish I had a dog treat in my pocket."

"You would have eaten it already," Ashley told her friend.

Lennon lifted his head. Flares of light accompanied by staccato bursts of gunfire split the silence. The soldiers caught sight of movement in the trees and fired indiscriminately. They advanced farther into the clearing, forming a circle to ensure the perimeter was covered. There was no sign of the ninjas. Or, the Keepers.

Lennon said to the girls, "Get down. Ashley's right. We fight. I'm going closer to see if I can help the Keepers. You stay here for now."

"I don't think so," Ashley replied. "We all go." She stood up.

"Change of plan." Lennon dragged her back down. "The soldiers have thermal imaging cameras mounted on their helmets. They don't need any light to see. The cameras pick up heat. As in, body heat."

The four scrunched together behind the flimsy log.

"What's the plan?" Ashley finally asked.

Lennon thought she was going to fold there for a while. Heck, he thought *he* was going to fold.

"The thermal imaging cameras will be picking up the heat of the Keepers' bodies everywhere. As soon as a Keeper pokes their head from around a tree trunk, those guys will spot it and shoot. If they look up, they'll see the Saskies and maybe the ravens. I don't know what the Keepers' plan is, but mine is to help them, even if I have to serve as a distraction. I think Omega's mission is to capture me and Ashley, and maybe a couple of Saskies, so they probably won't kill us on purpose."

"I don't hear a new plan in there," Jane mumbled.

"The problem is," Ashley said, "How can they tell our thermal images from the Keepers'?"

Lennon hadn't thought of that. He should stop underestimating Ashley. "They can't. Or tell our images from Jane's and Crystal's. The only option we have is to sneak up closer and wait. If we see a chance to take one of the enemy out, we do it.

Remember, we'll need to get in close. They have rifles and grenades and are trained in fighting with knives, so this isn't going to be easy."

A few scattered bursts of gunfire erupted from the clearing. A cry of pain followed, and Lennon hoped that it wasn't a Keeper.

"If we don't make it, "Ashley took Crystal's hand and reached out for Jane's, "remember that first star past the Milky Way. That's where we meet up." She turned to Lennon. "All four of us."

Lennon swallowed the lump in his throat. "Got it. Let's spread out and take cover behind a trunk. If you see a Keeper that needs help, do what you can."

As soon as the girls melted into the shadows, panic threatened to overwhelm Lennon. He made the wrong decision. They should have stayed together. He was a terrible Leader.

CHAPTER 43

DAGGER IN HAND, ASHLEY RAN left, keeping the clearing in sight. The mercenaries seemed reluctant to move farther into the forest. Maybe, they thought they were invincible, able to pick off the Keepers without threat to themselves. Did they know the Keepers had assault rifles, too? They must know the Keepers didn't possess the advantage of thermal imaging cameras and a grenade launcher.

She almost cried out in surprise when she passed a Keeper crouched behind a trunk, assault rifle aimed at the mercenaries. He — or, she — waved Ashley away, and she moved back farther into the darkness before continuing to circle. Now the clearing was barely illuminated, and it was difficult to keep it in sight. When the mercenaries moved deeper into the forest and discovered the Keepers, it was going to be a massacre. Lennon seemed to think he could help, but Ashley's goal was to keep him and her friends alive at all costs. She didn't want any harm to come to the Keepers but, bottom line, Ashley's new motto was: save your friends and yourself first.

When she could discern the figures of the mercenaries, she stopped and, copying the Keeper, crouched behind a giant trunk. Was it possible the mercenaries' thermal goggles couldn't detect the heat of humans through trees? There was so much she didn't know.

Ashley felt a tickling sensation in her mind. It wasn't Lennon. Thinking Jane or Crystal may have figured out how to telepath, she opened her mind to the incoming transmission.

It's Prin. Outgoing message to Lennon, Ashley, Crystal, and Jane. Do not approach a Keeper. They must focus on the enemy. If you remain behind a tree trunk, you cannot be detected by thermal imaging cameras.

The communication ceased. Creepy but useful. She reached out to Lennon, finding she could connect with a simple wish.

Did you hear Prin's message?

His response came immediately. *Yes. But, I don't know if Crystal and Jane heard.*

If you see them, tell them. What were the chances Ashley could locate her friends again in this black forest of horrors?

Her instincts urged her to move from tree to tree as far away as possible. Her conscience told her not to go without her friends, and she couldn't force herself to leave Lennon to fight on his own. She squatted behind a trunk and waited.

Gunfire erupted sporadically nearby. Ashley was soon able to differentiate between the sounds from the mercenaries' weapons and those of the Keepers. She heard a few more cries, cut short as the victims took cover to nurse their wounds. Or, to die.

Gee-zuz. Ashley turned and began to make her way back to the epicentre of the fighting. She reached the tree where the Keeper had shooed her away. He was still there. He snarled at her and waved his arm to send her away.

Before she had a chance to disappear, two figures landed beside her. The Keeper didn't react, but Ashley jumped a foot before recognizing Jane and Crystal. Well, she recognized their smell. Geez, she probably smelled the same, or worse.

"You guys! I could have stabbed you with my dagger."

"You'd need to have it in your hand first, girlfriend. Bottom line, we decided we're totally in." By Crystal's voice, she was hopping in place. "I know we're out-numbered and out-weaponed, but what choice do we have?"

Jane chimed in, "Yeah, we can't leave you and Lennon to beat up the enemy on your own."

The Keeper addressed them from behind a neighbouring tree. "Will you people kindly shut the hell up and make sure you don't give away our position?"

This was said in a hoarse baritone, and it was clear he was attempting to disguise his voice. Didn't fool Ashley this time, though. This was Fox Face who rode on the back of their truck. Recognition struck. She *knew* him.

Ashley pulled Jane and Crystal into a huddle. "Did you recognize that Keeper's voice? It's Fox, one of Prin's Guardians. Do you think he could be ... you know?"

"I'm thinking he is," Jane said in a low voice.

"Obviously," Crystal agreed.

The Keeper, aka He Who Should Never Be Named, darted around the tree, took aim and fired off a continuous round of ammo. A brief scream was followed by silence.

"Got the bastard," the Keeper announced with satisfaction.

Ashley and her friends relocated to another giant trunk, metres from the Keeper.

"Let's head out." Ashley said. "Time to face the dragon."

CHAPTER 44

THE WHITE RAVEN WITH THE black splotch dropped from the trees and landed on Lennon's shoulder. Instead of rubbing its beak against his cheek, it stared into his eyes. "No offence, bird, but you're going to give away my position."

The raven opened and closed its beak silently. Lennon guessed it didn't matter. The mercenaries could easily spot him in the dark with their cameras if he moved into the open, so what difference did it make if he had a white bird with him?

He looked down at the long, curved knife in his hand. It would be useless against weapons a thousand times more powerful wielded by the enemy. By the time he was close enough to use the knife, he would be shot and his dead body lying on the ground for the killer to walk over. Still, he didn't have any choice. No way would he surrender and be taken to some lab to be experimented on.

The raven uttered a squawk as a figure, then two more, closed in around him. This was it, time to die. He squatted, planning to plunge the blade into one attacker before it was lights out.

"Who's your friend?" Jane asked. "He's pooped on you again."

Lennon scarcely had time to lower his knife before Crystal wrapped her arms around his waist. "We thought you were already dead."

Ashley slid between her friends. "We did not. Don't be so dramatic, Crystal."

Lennon's heart beat a steady rhythm in his chest. Like some part of him calmed when they were all together. It seemed like days since they went their separate ways, not minutes. "How did you find me?"

"Who knows?" Ashley replied. "For some strange and annoying reason, I always know where you are."

"Get real already, Ash," Jane's voice sounded strained. "Like Prin said. You're Lennon's Protector. You two have a weird connection."

"We all do," Crystal added. "We're a Quartel."

Ashley pretended not to hear her friends. "Those guys are going to search the forest, one tree at a time. We can't evade them forever. We need to do something, and do it now."

Crystal craned her neck around the trunk and quickly pulled it back. "One of them is about twenty-five feet away and headed in this direction. He has the grenade launcher.'

"Get down," Lennon whispered. "Don't show your head again. We wait until he's right beside us, then we go in low. No mercy. He won't show us any."

"Oh god, oh god. We're dead." Crystal hyperventilated, and Lennon waited for it. He wasn't disappointed.

Ashley cuffed Crystal on the back of the head. "Knock it off. No time to go weak. Swing that hammer like you're freaking Thor, for crap's sake."

The gunfire in the forest abruptly ceased. For a short time, even the sounds of boots and weapons stilled but, all around, Lennon heard the rapid, adrenaline-laden breathing of a multitude of humans. He couldn't distinguish soldiers from Keepers. Above his head, branches shifted under the weight of heavy Saskie bodies. They better stay as quiet as possible.

The temporary silence broke when a burst of loud automatic gunfire erupted from the left, so close it had to be the lone soldier with the grenade launcher who had advanced close to their hiding spot.

Lennon whispered to the girls, "Crouch down and remember, go in low and hard. Wait until ..."

Another staccato surge of fire from a smaller weapon belonging to a Keeper preceded a scream that cut off in mid-pitch. Lennon heard a body hit the ground, and he sensed a life force snuff out. It was — just gone, with emptiness in its place. Great, was this another gift now, perceiving death?

The Keeper, weapon barrel pointed upward and the captured grenade launcher propped against his shoulder, appeared at his side.

"Okay, people, last time I'm going to tell you. Retreat into the forest. We have this section covered. Nobody's coming through. Go!"

Arms linked, Lennon and the girls skirted the Keeper and picked their way across the ground to the nearest trunk. The fighting resumed as they huddled together. A white blur soared across his peripheral vision and landed on his shoulder.

Lennon pressed his back against the bark. Maybe if he ignored it, the raven would go away for good. How had his life changed so drastically within a few short days? "Is it my imagination, or does that Keeper sound a lot like, you know ...?"

"It doesn't just sound like him; it is him," Crystal replied. "If I live through this, I'm never going to make fun of his funny hair and wrinkled suits again."

"Yeah, he's badass, but I see a round of detentions coming our way." Jane dropped to the ground but jumped up as soon as her rear end touched the frigid ground.

"Quiet," Ashley warned. "Someone's coming."

Lennon could have kicked himself. He should have been using his enhanced hearing instead of chit-chatting like he was already in detention and the monitor had stepped out to have a smoke.

Now, it was too late. A figure clad in body armour, helmet, heat-seeking goggles, and carrying a flame-thrower, stood between the quartet and any escape.

Uh, somebody should have mentioned there was a flame-thrower still in play.

"Gotcha," the soldier said, his voice low and rumbly. "Don't move a muscle, any of you, unless you want to be blasted into torches that will light up the sky for miles."

CHAPTER 45

ASHLEY MOVED IN FRONT OF the other three, but Lennon immediately stepped up beside her, shielding Jane and Crystal. The illumination from the light mounted on the soldier's helmet spread out into the forest beyond, but the knife Lennon held flat against his leg remained in shadow.

"You two ..." The soldier nodded at Lennon and Ashley. "You're coming with me. If you don't give me any trouble, I let the other two girls live." He rested the flame-thrower against his shoulder and pulled out a long-barrelled hand gun.

Ashley didn't believe him. He would kill her friends as soon as she and Lennon allowed him a clear shot. "Not happening."

The goon would notice if she reached for the dagger strapped to her back. Slowly, she extended two fingers into her pocket.

"Ash, we're done," Jane said. "If you and Lennon want to live, you have to go with him."

"This is not fair." Crystal's voice rang out. "We're only 16 and shouldn't have to die yet, not like this."

Ashley shoved Lennon aside until she stood in front. "I'm not going with him."

"Me neither," Lennon declared, pulling Ashley back until he was once again standing shoulder-to-shoulder with her.

The mercenary flung a string of profanities at them. "We're not having a discussion here, punks. I don't give a rat's ass what you want."

Ashley was struck by a sudden thought. Could she connect with the mind of this soldier-for-hire, hear what he was thinking? She knew from Prin that people who had the gift of magic could communicate with each other. But, could a magical person listen in to a non-magical mind? She projected her mind energy and connected with a jumble of fractured thoughts. Sorting quickly through the mess, she understood that he had been tasked with carrying the flame-thrower. He never expected to capture their prey.

With flame-thrower in one hand, and a gun in the other, his only option was to shoot. He was not supposed to kill or injure Lennon and Ashley, especially Lennon. He had no free hand to grab even one of them.

His momentary hesitation, while he struggled to

formulate a plan, allowed Ashley to extract the tiny weapon from her pocket and release the blade.

The confused mercenary remembered he had a communications line to his commander. He reached up to tap the "on" button with his gun hand.

Ashley dived low. Before his finger touched the button, she jammed her small blade into his unprotected calf. At the same time, Lennon leaped forward and swiped his knife across the man's gun hand. The weapon spun off into the forest. With a scream, the soldier collapsed onto his knees. The flame-thrower thudded to the ground.

The soldier's bloody fingers scrabbled after it but Crystal and Jane were on him. Crystal slammed her hammer against his helmet, knocking him backwards onto the ground. Jane pounded on the trigger mechanism of the flame-thrower with her hatchet, then dragged it away until Ashley lost sight of her. She waited anxiously until Jane popped out again.

Jane grinned at Ashley. "That takes care of that sucker."

A black-clad form darted out of the darkness and landed beside them. Crystal squeaked in alarm while Ashley drew her dagger from its sheath. In seconds, all four of them had their weapons pointed at the figure.

CHAPTER 46

"**LISTEN, PEOPLE. I'M NOT TELLING** you again. Find a place to hide and stay there!"

Fox bent and wrapped zip ties around the hands and ankles of the mercenary who was too stunned by Crystal's hammer attack on his helmet to fight back.

The Keeper picked up the hand gun and checked the safety was on. He tucked it into his waistband and dragged away his prize, calling to the teens, "We could have used that flame-thrower for our arsenal."

"Oops, sorry," Jane replied. To her friends she added, "Don't look directly into his eyes. That way, we can pretend we didn't recognize him."

Lennon urged the girls to follow him, and they fled deeper into the forest. The raven flew above them, tipping its wings to avoid the branches. The temperature had plummeted, and running warmed him up. He halted behind a colossal trunk that looked like every other Sitka spruce in the forest. The girls slammed into each other, holding their sides and gasping.

Before he dialed his sight back to normal to give his eyeballs a rest, Lennon saw puffs of their breath float outward and disappear into the bark of the old growth giant. He placed his hand over the spot on the bark. His body trembled as he absorbed the energies of the three girls and the tree. Every living thing on earth really was connected.

A frost-laden breeze drifted through the trees, carrying the scent of firs and earth, and something else. A human smell ...

He'd just screwed up again, losing focus when he should have been super alert. He should not have turned down his super senses. Before he had time to open his mouth to warn the girls or try and discern the source of the danger smell, a black-clad figure entered his range of sight.

This time, it wasn't a Keeper. Lennon herded the girls together behind him, but it was too late.

"Gee-zuz, it's one of those real ninjas." Ashley voice whispered in his ear.

"Crappity-crap." Crystal raised her hammer and stepped forward, only to be jerked aside by Jane who brandished her hatchet over their heads. Since Jane was the shortest of the four, the hatchet came too close to the heads of her friends for their comfort. Ashley grabbed Jane's hatchet hand and lowered it.

Lennon utilized his enhanced hearing but couldn't sense the ninja's three friends. The rustling in the branches above his head wasn't made from the light-footed ninjas. He hoped the Sasquatch family could keep their kids quiet, or they would for sure find themselves in an Omega lab.

The ninja threw a switch on a head lamp, and the teens were suddenly bathed in a bright light.

"Enough of this nonsense." The ninja moved his head to highlight each face before returning to Lennon. "You, Lennon, will come with me. The blonde girl too. The way she fights, she has magic potential. No more games. The other two can scamper off into the woods and wait to be rescued in a day or two."

As if they hadn't heard that before, like, just a few minutes ago.

The man's voice was muffled by the black cloth wrapped around his lower face, yet the voice resonated in Lennon's head. He'd heard it before. Was it something to do with his fangs?

The ninja fighter held the familiar gun that resembled a Taser but was really a tranquilizer delivery weapon. Lennon didn't care to be hit with that thing again. Pretty sure Ashley didn't, either.

Buying time in case a Keeper was near and could help them, Lennon asked the man, "Where are your three buddies? You won't be able to carry two unconscious bodies out on your own."

"If you'll co-operate, I won't have to tranquilize you. Hoping you'll both see reason and come quietly. As far as my cohorts go, they're either dead or captured. Doesn't matter. I've got things under control. If you give me trouble, I'll kill the three girls and just take you. You're the main prize. Now, all of you drop your toy weapons."

Ashley sent a telepathic message to Lennon and included her friends, hoping they would hear it. *He can't get us all with that thing. Whoever's still standing, take him down.*

Four against one, Ash. We got this. Crystal!

As if he'd sensed their intent to try and stop him, an evil-looking gun appeared in the ninja's other hand. "A semi-automatic Beretta." His voice was stony. "Very effective. And accurate."

Slowly, one by one, dagger, hatchet, hammer, and knife hit the ground at the ninja's feet.

"Quite the choice," Ashley observed.

Her cold fingers brushed against Lennon's hand. He linked his fingers with hers and squeezed them. Above his head, branches thrashed wildly. A dark-brown, baby Saskie dropped to the ground at their feet and lay stunned before staring up at the ninja. She — or he — cried out in fright before scrambling to her feet and turning to run.

"Hey, you, get back here!" the ninja roared. "You're coming with me."

Recognition slammed into Lennon. His fingers flew to the back of his neck to touch the injection site which had swollen into a hot lump.

"That's your dentist," Ashley whispered into his ear. Lennon waited for her signature jab in the ribs but it never came.

"Dr. Clemens!" Lennon accused. The bump on his neck throbbed like a yellow jacket sting.

Two adult Saskies landed between the ninja and the terrified baby. The six-foot parents crouched on their haunches in attack mode, claws extending from their stubby fingers. They growled deep in their chests, the warning sound feral cats make before ripping out the throats of their prey.

The tranquilizer gun and the Beretta waved between the parents and the baby, then back to the four teens. Dr. Clemens couldn't decide which weapon to use, bullets or tranquilizers.

Without conscious thought, Lennon connected to Dr. Clemens' mind and knew he was going to use his gun to kill the adult Saskies. All three girls would meet the same fate. Then the dentist would turn the tranquilizer device on Lennon and the baby. He thought he could carry both out.

Before Lennon's super speed could react to the threat, Crystal shouted, "You are a bad, bad dentist."

A half second later, her hammer soared by Lennon's ear and hit Dr. Clemens on the shoulder. The man fell to his knees but remained in possession of his weapons. He aimed one at the teens and the other at the Saskies.

CHAPTER 47

JANE'S MIND STRANDS REACHED OUT to Ashley. *Remember our switchblades.* Crystal would receive the same message.

The hammer-blow to the shoulder jarred the dentist's head lamp off when his knees hit the ground. He made no attempt to retrieve it, holding his weapons steady. The tranquilizer device didn't seem as threatening in comparison to the killing capacity of the Beretta.

Ashley yanked her mini-switchblade from her pocket and shoved Lennon aside. She kicked Dr. Clemens' weapon out of his right hand, hoping it was the Beretta. She'd lost track.

At the same instant, Lennon reached out to grab the dentist's left hand. To Ashley, it looked like Lennon barely twisted the wrist, but the weapon —

the tranquilizer gun, she could see now — slammed against the tree trunk. The man cried out and slumped over as his hand hung limply from the damaged wrist.

All four teens piled onto Dr. Clemens, with Ashley and her two BFFs wielding their small blades. He was muscular, tough to pin down. They rolled him over onto his stomach and Jane stomped on the fingers of his right hand as he scrambled to locate one of his weapons. She bent over and stabbed the hand. He shouted in anger and pain and continued to thrash wildly, refusing to give up.

Crystal hooked an arm under the man's chin and yanked his head backwards. The black cloth looped around his head and face came off in her hand. Flinging it aside, she tightened her arms around his bald head. His struggles loosened her grip, causing the switchblade to slip from her fingers. "Asshat dentist." Crystal grabbed his prominent ears and used them as handles to slam his forehead into the ground. She picked up her blade and lightly drew it across the top of his hairless head. Just deep enough to cause two thin lines of blood to well up in the shape of an X. "How does that feel, evil ninja?"

He roared promises of torture and death, his threats flying at them like sharp tacks.

Ashley balanced on the man's shoulders, switchblade ready. "Go ahead, jerkface. Move and I'll carve you a new belly button. On your back."

"Really, Ash? Belly button?" Jane gave her a disgusted look. "Is that the best you got?"

"I'm tired, okay?" Ashley shot back. "I should just poke his eyeballs out right now, but that would be kind of gross while he watches me."

Bleeding from his forehead and right hand, the other hand broken and useless from Lennon's twist, Dr. Clemens attempted to wiggle his head from Crystal's clutches. She picked up her hammer and gave him a slight tap in the middle of the X incision. He bucked frantically to throw Ashley off his back. Every time he dug the fingers of his bloodied hand into the cold earth to lever himself to his knees, Jane grinded the hand flat under her feet and jabbed at his fingers.

Ashley looked behind her at Lennon. He had picked up his curved knife and was sitting on the ninja-dentist's legs, his head bent slightly to one side, the same pose she had seen Prin adopt when she listened for a telepathic transmission. Lennon's raven fluttered down and perched on his shoulder. The Saskie family had disappeared into the safety of the primeval forest.

Dr. Clemens decided resistance wasn't working, so he tried reasoning. "Listen, you kids. You don't understand what a privilege is being offered here. You have the opportunity to take part in a study that will benefit all mankind. The virus that Omega released a few months ago to a select number of subjects didn't go as planned, and that's why we need Lennon. We want to determine why a few individuals didn't lose their heightened abilities. You, blonde girl, seem to have some of these aptitudes as well, so we ..."

"Don't care." Ashley retrieved her dagger and slammed the hilt down on the ninja/dentist's head — yup, in the middle of the X. He fell silent and she looked at her weapon in astonishment. Did she really just knock this loon unconscious?

Lennon gave her a disapproving glance. "He was telling us stuff."

"We learned that Omega is responsible for the LM43 virus. Maybe, the Keepers can interrogate him for more details. We can't let this guy get away when he wakes up, so help me find something we can use to tie him up."

A volley of ravens shot from the trees and landed on the ground One bird hopped close to the unconscious dentist and surveyed the bloody X before turning its beady, blue eyes on the teens. In Ashley's exhausted mind, it appeared the raven was thinking, *what the hell is up with you kids?*

Prin's voice called out to them, "Thank you, guys, we can take it from here." Like wisps of smoke rising from a campfire, Prin's Quartel emerged from the shadows into the dimming light of Dr. Clemens' head lamp.

CHAPTER 48

PRIN WAS ACCOMPANIED BY HER Protector, Frog, and her Guardians, Mouse and the other one Ashley pretended to not notice. Although, with strands of his out-of-control hair rimming the eye holes of his ski-mask, he was hard to ignore. *Awkward!*

"Good job," Prin said. "We've neutralized the enemy and have some prisoners to transport to headquarters." She prodded the unconscious dentist with her toe. "Anyone got zip ties?"

Frog secured the dentist and slung him over his shoulder. Ashley eyed the tall, heavily-muscled Protector. Proof positive she couldn't be Lennon's Protector even if she wanted to, which she didn't, big time. She was nowhere near this guy's level of training or physical strength. Opting out was the right decision.

"Now, we're really getting out of here." Prin looked into the treetops where the branches creaked louder than the cold breeze. She spoke in the Saskie language and stood back as two adults and two juveniles dropped to the ground. They fell in line behind the Keepers, leaving the teens at the end. A dozen ravens flew in and out of sight. Their powerful wingbeats concealed the sound of human footfalls.

As they headed through the winter forest, brittle pine needles crackled under their feet. Was Ashley living through an unending time loop? Who didn't like trees? Right now, though, she was sick of the sight of them. She wanted to get home and take a shower. Then grab a hamburger. And poutine.

At least this time they weren't running. The Keepers set a leisurely pace and talked quietly to each other.

"Psst. Hey." Jane jogged up between Lennon and Ashley. "Do you think what's-his-name will cut us some slack and let us skip first class so we can sleep in?"

Ashley peered ahead and decided the Keepers couldn't hear them if they spoke in low tones. "Nope. But if he goes on this week-long trip to the wilderness to re-locate the Saskies, he won't know if we show up or not."

Crystal spoke from behind. "He can look at attendance records. Maybe we can ask him if we can be excused."

Lennon grunted. "Why don't we keep pretending we don't recognize him? That's a better plan."

"I agree." Ashley preferred to forget this whole trip, especially since she wasn't going to join the Keepers.

"We need a code name for him," Crystal announced. "So we can refer to him and nobody knows who we're talking about. We can't use his Keeper name, Fox, for security reasons."

"Sure, Crys," Ashley responded. "From now on, he's Attila." That should prevent the gang from coming up with a stupid name like Fluff-Bunny or Rambo.

There was some grumbling between Jane and Crystal, but eventually it was agreed. Attila. Lennon kept up his steady pace behind the Keepers and didn't contribute to the conversation. Ashley reached out to his mind but met with resistance.

Fine. Maybe he was thinking about his options. Join the Keepers and find himself a new Protector, or decline the invitation and go back to being a regular kid. Like her.

CHAPTER 49

LENNON PERCEIVED THE SOFT PROD of Ashley's mind as she tried to connect with him. It was mean, not allowing her access, but he needed to think about a few things. It was cool that all three of the girls were able to communicate telepathically now. He still hadn't figured out how to "speak" to one person and not have others overhear. Not for sure. It seemed to have something to do with intent, like magic in general.

A sharp poke to the middle of his back interrupted his musings. Damn that finger, anyway.

"Lennon, we need to discuss a few things."

Lennon didn't stop walking. "Like what?"

Ashley scurried after him, and her voice came so close to his ear, he jumped and dislodged the white raven getting a free ride on his shoulder. It squawked once, then regained its perch.

"Like, if you're going to become a Keeper, you have to find a Protector that isn't me."

Lennon's heart clenched in his chest. "But, we're a Quartel. Prin said so."

"Becoming a Keeper is a choice. And I choose not. I want to do normal things, like go to University and have a family someday. Not get shot at, and threatened, and dragged around unconscious, and — and ..."

"But, Ash." Crystal's voice broke. "We're a team."

"I can't do it," Ashley responded. "Sorry, it's not for me."

Jane pushed her way forward. "Crystal and I aren't strong enough to be Protectors. We have your backs, and we can fight when we have to, but you're faster and have better instincts. If you can't be the Protector, then none of us can be Keepers."

Until this moment, Lennon didn't realize how much he wanted to be a Keeper, to be special, to help the world keep going, even when it seemed to be falling apart.

A lumbering figure emerged from the forest. Hank, still wearing his brown, padded coat and plaid hat, draped a thick arm across Lennon's shoulder. "Hi, buddy, where've you been?"

"Mrphh!" Hank hugged him so hard, Lennon felt his bones crunch. The raven screeched and hopped onto Hank's head.

After a few minutes of wordless marching, Lennon spoke to the girls. "It's true. We can't do this without Ashley. We have to be all in it, or it won't work." He meant what he said, but depression enveloped him when none of the girls responded.

They reached a small clearing. From shards of moonlight shining through the branches, Lennon saw the dull glint of metal. They had reached the personnel carriers.

Several powerful flashlights clicked on. The shadows cast by sentinel Keepers loomed over the bound bodies of soldiers, stripped of their weapons and hi-tech devices.

The bodies lay limp on the ground. Were they dead? A shadow bent and the sound of tearing duct tape reached them as the Keeper plastered the tape over the mouths of the captives.

"Gave them a little taste of their own medicine," Prin said, the satisfaction in her voice overriding her fatigue. "They won't wake up for twelve hours at least. By then, we'll have dropped them off over headquarters on the way to our destination."

At Crystal's sharp intake of breath, she added, "We're not animals. We'll put parachutes on them first, of course, with a timed device to open the parachutes before they hit the ground. Our interrogation experts can take it from there."

Lennon did a head count of the prisoners. Six mercenaries plus the newest captive, Dr. Evil Dentist.

"What about the others ...?" There had been a dozen soldiers at least, and three other ninja fighters.

Prin didn't answer him. She turned to her Protector. "I want a clean-up crew in the area as soon as possible. The bodies of the loggers in the crater are to be taken back to their camp where they can be found by the logging company. Their families deserve to know. The dead Omega mercenaries and ninjas should be collected and placed in the helicopters. No need for hikers or park personnel to come across rotting corpses in the spring."

"What about the dog?" asked one of the Keepers. "The sedative should keep him under for at least 12 hours as well."

Prin was silent for a minute. "Tell the clean-up crew to drop the dog off at a mainland shelter. Not on the island. No telling if the animal has been embedded with a tracking device and we haven't got time to scan the dog and remove it. Now, I know we're short on space, and I want the captured weapons and assorted devices added to our inventory at the new site. No option but to secure the Omega employees to the hoods of the trucks. Don't stack them so high the drivers can't see where they're going."

The darkness prevented Lennon from counting the shadows milling around, lifting the prisoners from the ground and dragging them around to the front of the trucks. Prin kept up a running rat-a-tat of orders and, before Lennon could interject his question regarding any casualties among the Keepers, the four teens were again loaded into the first truck before it backed out onto the forest road.

Lennon sat across from the girls, with Prin on one side of him, and Hank on the other. The raven left Hank's head to stand with one claw on Hank's shoulder, the other on Lennon's.

Please pick Hank, Lennon pleaded silently.

CHAPTER 50

ASHLEY FOLDED HER ARMS AND leaned her head against the wall of the truck. The vibration of the vehicle jarred her teeth, and she massaged her neck. How much longer would this nightmare last? Her friends were disappointed in her but, gee-zuz, it was her life, her right not to spend it pursued by bad guys. At least the amorous Saskie from the first truck ride had been relegated to a seat at the end of the bench.

The toddler perched on Jane's knee reached over and touched a strand of Ashley's hair. Ashley took the little hand in hers, feeling the soft padding of the palm. One day soon, the pad would become tough from the effort of swinging from branch to branch and hanging onto the coarse bark. The Saskie slid onto her lap and Ashley put her arms around the fuzzy creature. Not that its fur smelled that great, but the little one was warm and comforting, like a teddy bear.

"We're almost at our destination," Prin announced. "So, listen up."

Ashley jabbed her elbow into Jane's ribs and struggled to focus on Prin. If another crisis was coming up, she vowed to climb a tree with the Saskies and wait for whatever to happen. Not caring anymore was kind of calming.

In the pitch black of the truck, she couldn't see her friends but, if they were half as wasted as her, they weren't up for another fight either.

"Is everyone awake?" Prin asked.

Ashley grunted and heard three varying sounds of assent. Apparently satisfied she had a conscious audience, Prin continued.

"Don't think that today was a typical Keeper field trip. We are seldom called upon to fight armed militia and trained ninjas. Most of our battles occur in the courts and board rooms. However, all Keepers must train for these occurrences. I suspect as world chaos ramps up, our fighting skills will be required more frequently. Fortunately, we didn't lose anyone today. You four conducted yourselves well the past few days. If you decide to become Keepers, we'll welcome you gladly."

Trying to clear the frog out of her throat, Ashley made a honking sound, much like a Canada goose at the back end of the V, afraid of being left behind. Awkward, much? She turned the honk into a cough.

"But that is a choice we can't let you make for a few years yet. As I mentioned before, you are a natural Quartel — Leader, Protector, two Guardians — but that's a fluid term. One or more of you may opt out and the position will be filled by someone else. There are other young magicals who will need to become part of a group. In the meantime, if you have an interest in becoming a Keeper someday, my advice is to train relentlessly and choose your career paths wisely. Keepers need to take time off without notice quite frequently, so it's good to have a job with flexible vacation days. We will be there for you when you need assistance."

"Uh, does this mean we can't have kids? I plan to be a botanist, but might like a family someday." Trust Crys to get to the important stuff.

"Of course, you can have a family." Prin opened the flap and allowed an icy current of air to blow through the space. Saskies and humans alike sucked in fresh air as Prin asked Frog to climb in.

"Yeah, right," Ashley mumbled. "Like there's room." The toddler lay heavy in her arms, fast asleep and hotter than a tiny furnace.

Frog squatted on the floor in front of Prin. "Five minutes out, pet. Plane is fuelled and ready to go as soon as we load."

Ashley listened with interest. What's this? Pet?

243

"Frog is not only my Protector. He's my husband, and we have three children."

Words gathered in Ashley's brain faster than her mouth could spill them. "Wha...? You're marr...? Say, wh...?" She tried again. "The Leader and the Protector have to get married?" Even though she couldn't see Lennon, she knew right where to aim her scowl.

Prin and Frog laughed.

"Certainly not," Prin said, the mirth evident in her tone. "But it happens sometimes. It makes it easier all around if a Keeper pairs up with another Keeper, but it's not a requirement."

Jane and Crystal — and Lennon — were suspiciously quiet, which meant — what, exactly?

"We're almost there," Prin said, "so are there any questions?"

Ashley had a million, but since none of the answers would affect her future, she contented herself with one. "Lennon lives in an abandoned building with not much in the way of support, financial or emotional. How is he supposed to train to be a good fighter, let alone get an education?"

"Hey," Lennon began. "I can look after myself."

"Excellent question, Ashley," Prin responded. "Lennon is going to move into a group home out of the foster system. He'll have a chance to meet other magical teens who need acceptance and support. We'll help him find a part-time job so he can maintain his current independence without jeopardizing his future. We'll get him a cell phone, too."

"You can make that happen?" Crys sounded surprised. It was odd not to hear the constant clacking from the beads. Ashley kind of missed that sound although she would never admit it out loud.

"Not to sound immodest," Prin replied, "but our global organization has amassed a fortune over the millennia. Think Knights Templar treasure. It's not a myth, guys. One of our objectives is to ensure that latent Keepers reach their full potential. Lennon will receive everything he needs to move forward. The same with you girls. If you need help, we're here. No strings. In the end, if any or all of you decide not to become Keepers, well, that's our loss but it happens. In any case, we won't leave Lennon in his present situation. Does that answer your question, Ashley?"

Prin shifted in her seat, and Ashley sensed that the Leader and her Protector were leaning against each other. "Guess so," she mumbled.

Although she wasn't ready to admit it, Ashley was having second thoughts about law as a profession. Boring, or what?

CHAPTER 51

LENNON JERKED HIS CHIN FROM his chest. How long before he could rest on his worn-out hospital bed? Without an alarm, he had trained himself to wake up at 7 a.m. each morning but would his exhausted mind work tomorrow? Right now, he didn't care.

"Changing the subject to keep the conversation going so I can stay awake," Jane said, "how did Omega track us? It's like they knew where we were going before we did."

"Tell them, Lennon." Ashley instructed. "Or, I will."

"The ninjas rode on the roof of our boxcar." Lennon tasted a familiar resentment at Ashley's order. He was supposed to be the Leader. You didn't hear Frog barking instructions at Prin.

"Before that," Ashley prompted. "And, you didn't tell me about the ninjas on the roof."

"Dr. Clemens injected me in the neck with a tranquilizer when I was in his office to get my fangs filed down. I think he implanted a tracker on me." The inflamed lump on Lennon's neck throbbed in unison with his heartbeat.

"Well, shit, lad." Frog yanked Lennon's head forward, shining a flashlight on the site of the injection. "Infected, and definitely a tracking device in there. Our airport location is compromised."

The rumble of the engine roared louder, then cut off. The shaking stilled as the personnel carriers came to a stop.

"We've reached our destination," Prin called in a nasal parody of the annoying GPS lady. "Everyone out. You four stand to one side, but don't leave. We have to get the tracker out of Lennon. This will be our last visit to this airport. We'll have to find a new one in case Omega is still monitoring the tracker from a remote location."

"Ah, I think I'll go to the ER once we're back in Victoria," Lennon began, suddenly wide awake.

"Nope. This is a security thing. Just as we have people in every walk of life, Omega spies are everywhere. Frog is a paramedic. He'll have that tracker out in a jiffy." Prin added, "It'll be over before you know it."

Lennon had heard that before and, here he was,

wasted, beat to hell, and chipped like the family dog. Not exactly the best time of his life. He didn't want to walk around with a bulls-eye on his neck, so he didn't resist as Frog sat him on the cold tarmac and set to work swabbing his neck with disinfectant.

"Sorry, lad, this won't take long. First, I have to clean the area. There a lot of dirt on your neck."

Like he had to announce that to everyone? The girls stood over him and observed Frog pry the tracker from under his skin. He'd experienced worse pain than this and sat silently. Frog let out a triumphant sound and held out the tweezers so Lennon could see. Lennon's super eyesight noted a pebble-like item that dripped blood and ... was that pus?

Prin took the tweezers from Frog and handed it to another Keeper. "I've never seen anything quite like this. I'd like to have it reverse-engineered, but it's too risky to keep around. Take photos of it for our scientists, then smash it, and scatter the dust around the landing strip."

"Lennon is supposed to have an accelerated healing ability," Ashley said to Prin. "Why is the injection site so gross and not healed over?"

"His body is rejecting a foreign object and trying to heal an infection at the same time. In a few more days, I've no doubt he'd never know it was there."

Lennon rested his head on his raised knees as Frog placed a bandage over the wound. He was a bit dizzy from fatigue and lack of food but wasn't going to admit it in front of the girls. And, that wasn't leadership, it was survival. Their regular hovering was bad enough. If he showed weakness, they would follow him everywhere until the end of time.

Through a haze of exhaustion, Lennon heard Prin's voice. "I've been in touch with our surgeon. He suggested a broad-spectrum, dual antibiotic and antifungal shot for all of you, and a supplemental oral course for Lennon. We'll need a blood sample after three days to determine if more treatment is required. Now, who's first? Lennon? Any allergies?"

CHAPTER 52

ASHLEY WATCHED THE TRANSPORT PLANE bank north and disappear into the night sky. The farewell scene between Lennon and Hank had been gut-wrenching but, gee-zuz, Prin had invited them all to spend next summer working at the new sanctuary, so he would be re-united with his friend in a few months.

He had a new friend, anyway. Ashley stifled a giggle at the sight of the white raven with the black-splotched chest sitting on Lennon's shoulder. The rest of the ravens had flown without hesitation into the hold of the plane after the Saskies.

"What are you going to call your raven?" she asked Lennon.

Lennon looked straight ahead. "I'm not naming him. He's probably sorry already that he isn't on that plane because I'm not feeding him. There's probably a no-pet rule at my new group home."

"Not likely," Crystal told him. "Prin said there will be other magicals at your new place. They might have animal familiars, too, like black cats or frogs. Won't it be neat if there's a house elf to do all the cooking and cleaning? Like Dobby?"

"Get a grip, Crys." Jane slapped her friend across the arm. "No such things as fairies, or elves, or ..."

"Just like there's no such things as enchanted forests, and wards, and Keepers and Sasquatches?" Much as Ashley would like to believe these past few days were a weird dream, like one caused by inhaling spores from hallucinogenic mushrooms, this was reality. Her *new* reality.

She tried to keep track of the Keepers during the loading and takeoff. As near as she could determine, seven Keepers, including Prin and her Protector slash husband (and, wasn't that just too bizarre) had taken off for the week-long journey to the remote new home of the Saskies.

The remaining three Keepers drove the battered military trucks into a neat line at the edge of the tarmac. They slashed the tires, yanked wires loose under the hoods, and left the vehicles to rust.

Two of the remaining Keepers prepared to depart in an SUV missing its back bumper. In the brief moment of light when the driver opened the door and pulled off his ski mask, Ashley recognized the coronet of wild, curly hair. "Oops. Didn't see that."

She stood with her friends and watched the vehicle disappear along a dirt track into the winter gloom. Soon, not even the tail lights were visible.

Jane's phone lit up. "Hey, we have bars. Well, one bar. It's 5:37 in the p.m."

"Super," Crystal responded. "Maybe we can call a taxi. As if. Where are we anyway?"

Ashley surveyed their surroundings. Or she would have, if there was any light beyond Jane's cell phone. Total darkness as far as her eye could see. She couldn't even make out the pot-holed tarmac beneath her feet. Talk about a death trap. "I thought the Keepers were going to take us home? Kind of harsh, leaving us alone in the middle of who-the-hell-knows."

Lennon jostled her elbow. "We can't be too far outside Victoria."

"Not helpful. I never heard of an abandoned air strip close to Victoria, have you?"

"No."

"I can't walk another freaking step. We've been gone less than 48 hours, and do you know how many hours of sleep I've had? Do you?" Ashley felt hysteria rising and was going to let it out. She didn't care who witnessed her meltdown. And, was it *snowing*?

"None?" Lennon shifted feet and pulled back on the collar of his jacket to ease the pressure on his wound. "But, to be fair, time was different inside the ward, so we probably didn't need to sleep."

Fat snowflakes melted on Ashley's heated cheeks as she peered up into his face. "Don't tell me I don't need sleep. Just figure out how we're going to get out of here. You're supposed to be the freaking Supreme Leader of this freaking *Quartel*." She gave him a shove. "So, lead!"

Jane stepped between them. "Take it easy, Ash. We'll get out of here. Remember, you're his Protector and have to be the toughest warrior. And, look, it's snowing!"

Ashley groaned and darted into the inky darkness until she could just barely make out Jane's cell light. "I am *not* his Protector! And, being a warrior mostly just *sucks*!" She was sick of feeling responsible for Lennon and Jane and Crystal. Her chaotic thoughts reminded her of entering the mind of the mercenary with the flame thrower. What a shit show it was in there. Maybe she'd tell her friends about that annoying ability; maybe she wouldn't bother.

A movement from behind her caused her to whirl around. Before she could extract her dagger from her back holster, a calm voice halted her movement.

"Why don't we see about getting you guys home?"

Once again, the voice was familiar. And, this time Ashley knew exactly who it was.

A blur that was Crystal rushed by Ashley and threw herself at the newcomer. "Peter!"

Master Peter Li wore the black fitted clothing

of the Keepers. A folded cloak lay over his arm and a white mask dangled from one finger. Ashley was never so relieved in her life.

"I hoped I could remain anonymous, but we decided you may be more inclined to take your fighting lessons seriously if you know I'm a Keeper. Lennon, too, of course."

Master Li looked directly at Lennon. "You're a natural fighter, but you need formal training. You would benefit greatly from my Wednesday evening mixed taekwondo class for males and the Saturday morning Krav Maga training I've devised for these three young women."

Noting Lennon's hesitation, Master Li added, "Free for you, of course. All fees covered by the Keeper foundation."

Right now, Ashley just wanted to go home. "Do you have your car, Master Li? Can you drive us back to Victoria?"

He bowed. "Certainly, Ashley. But, first, we are going to stop at my gym. While you shower, I will wash and dry your clothes. I don't know what your parents would think if you arrive home in this condition."

They certainly wouldn't think their children had been lost in a time warp for two days, been chased by two batches of bad guys — and one good batch — kidnapped, cuddled by Sasquatches, and fought for their lives more than once.

"Good idea," Ashley said. "Come on, guys. Let's get out of here."

She jerked to a stop and twisted to face Master Li. "You're Padded Jacket, aren't you? The man who followed us from Dr. Clemens' office and fought off that ninja."

"All part of our protection services." Master Li herded them into a non-descript dark Caravan, turned on the wipers against the falling snow, and headed through the forest on a one-lane, unpaved road. "We'll have better cell reception in a few minutes. You can call your parents and tell them the usual lies about where you've been for two days."

Master Li kept his window cracked on the journey to Victoria.

CHAPTER 53

IN THE FORMER SANCTUARY, THE majestic Douglas fir and Sitka spruce shivered. But, warned of impending temperature changes by the Keepers, they quickly adapted. By using the fungal network that connected their root systems, the stronger trees shared energy and nutrients with those younger or weaker, ensuring the community survived the cold months ahead.

The ferns fell into winter sleep, ready to rise green and lush in the spring, while the flowers stopped blooming out of season, conserving energy and waiting for slivers of April sun to warm them awake again.

The animals returned. First came a lone cougar, then deer, wolves, a bear, and a herd of elk. They trod hesitantly across the cooling ground, aware that the long, unnatural summer had ended. Some looked high overhead at the branches, searching for the white birds and the elusive, human-like creatures that sometimes lumbered through the forest, taking to the trees to sleep and to avoid danger. Detecting no signs of the enchantment that drove them away when they were very young, the animals grew emboldened. Dozens more crossed the threshold to the land where they had been born, bringing with them many seasons of offspring.

Hours after the Keepers and the future Keepers lowered the magical shield, the Sanctuary was gone, re-absorbed into the natural rhythm of the woodland. And, visible only to those that could see beyond the ordinary, the glowing energy remnants of loggers, armed soldiers, and ninja warriors joined the trappers and First Nations people on their never-ending journeys across the forest floor.

Monday morning. Never a good time, but hell on earth for the teens this week. Lennon stayed on at the gym the night before, sleeping on a cot provided by Master Li in the men's dressing room. The white raven nestled in a towel on the floor beside him. Once the girls were clean and dry, Master Li called a taxi and instructed the driver to let them off at the three separate addresses he provided. No substitutions.

Monday morning assembly in the Vic High auditorium found the foursome still exhausted and sporting a colourful array of bruises and scrapes. Lennon wore a hoody that mostly covered his neck wound, almost healed. They had scored seats in the very back row and slouched so that only the tops of their heads showed above the seats in front.

Ashley passed her phone to Lennon. On the screen was a photo of him leaning against a Sitka, his arm around Hank's shoulders. The Sasquatch wore his brown jacket and trapper hat. "When you get a phone, I'll send you a copy."

Lennon found it difficult to speak for a moment. He cleared his throat. "Thanks."

"No biggie," Ashley said, shrugging. "Hey, I wonder if Fox will be here."

"Of course, he's going to be here," Jane whispered. "He didn't leave on the plane. We saw him drive away. And, I thought we were going to call him by the code name, Attila?"

Ashley was sick of keeping track of multiple names for the Keepers, this one in particular — Fox Face, Attila. "It's Mr. Langster, for crap's sake. Brad Langster. Just don't make eye contact. He'll go back to his office after, and we can avoid him for the rest of the day."

"What about the rest of semester?" Lennon asked. "And next semester, and next year?"

"What's the big deal?" Without beads to contain

her braids, Crystal had gathered her long, black hair into a bun and stabbed it into submission with two long spikes that looked like her grandma's knitting needles. "We know he's a Keeper. He knows we know."

"It's weird is all," Jane mumbled. "What if he expects us to get better marks or something?"

Lennon and Ashley looked at each other and laughed.

"Pretty sure he doesn't expect us do anything except become Keepers someday," Crystal said.

"He's still the principal," Jane countered stubbornly.

Crystal pointed to the front of the auditorium. "There he is. Mr. Langster. Underneath that wrinkled suit and crazy hair, he's a total rebel." She sat up straight. "Let's practise mind-speak. We can talk to each other anytime we want, even if we don't have cell reception."

"Not a good idea," Lennon warned. "Mr. Langster might be able to listen in. We better learn the rules first, like is there a radial distance, or can telepathy travel across the world, depending on who we're trying to contact?"

Ashley refrained from rolling her eyes. She was trying to break the habit. "Mind-speak has something to do with intent, like all magic, but I agree it's best to wait and find out. Maybe Master Li can fill us in."

Jane clutched Ashley's arm. "You said 'us', Ash.

Does this mean you're going to be one of us — potential Keepers?"

Ashley examined her friends' intent expressions. "Maybe. I don't know yet. We only just found out about the Keepers and what they do. I can't make a decision that will affect my whole life, like overnight." She avoided looking at the guy sitting five rows down, second from the left. Would Devon ask her out again after she stood him up Saturday night? Hah, no.

Lennon watched patiently while Ashley pulled her lip gloss from her pocket and coated her lips. When she was done, he asked, "Will you at least come with us to work at the new sanctuary this summer? We'll see Hank again and the other Sasquatches." He really didn't want any other Protector. He'd rather have Ashley watching his back than anyone else, even if she was snarky at times. She didn't seem to mind his raven, and Lennon felt in his bones that he was stuck with the bird.

"Yeah. I'm going to do that. It'll be a good experience for me, no matter what I decide to do with the rest of my life. But, I promise nothing more than that." Ashley wouldn't mind seeing the Sasquatches again and couldn't imagine a whole summer without her friends. She'd even miss Lennon, for whatever reason. Because, she had to admit that he was a friend now, same as Jane and Crystal.

Jane reached over and thumped Ashley's thigh

with her fist, while Lennon squeezed her arm. Crystal whispered, "The Victoria Quartel is ready for our first mission! Almost."

"So, what'd you really name your raven?" Ashley asked Lennon.

"Smudge," he admitted.

A roar erupted from the stage. Mr. Langster pointed his finger at the back row. "Will you people kindly sit up and shut up? See me in my office after the assembly."

Every kid in the auditorium turned around in their seats and snickered at the four losers marked for detention.

"Should be fun," Ashley whispered to Lennon.

The end.

ACKNOWLEDGEMENTS

My thanks yet again to Donna Warner for her editing proficiency. Her assistance with Blood Shield was, as usual, invaluable.

My everlasting gratitude to Donna Houghton and Alyssa MacPherson, my enthusiastic and stalwart beta readers whose comments and suggestions made this book turn out a whole lot better!

Special thanks to Maureen Langford, who generously read the manuscript twice – once as a beta reader and then again as a proof-reader. So, any errors are hers. (Just kidding! Any errors are my fault as usual.)

Thank you to M.J. Moores of Infinite Pathways for ensuring the cover design perfectly matches Book 1, BLOOD PATCH.

Love and thanks to Olyvia, who gave me important insight into teen culture.

Finally, a huge shout-out to my writing group, the Genre5 – Donna Warner, DL Houghton, Pam Blance and Liz Lindsay (Pam & Liz write as crime author Jamie Tremain). Thank you for the support, the advice and, most of all, the many years of laughter. I couldn't do this without you!

CHECK OUT THESE OTHER BOOKS BY

GLORIA FERRIS

The BLOOD YA urban Fantasies

BLOOD PATCH
BLOOD SHIELD

The Cornwall and Redfern Mysteries:

CORPSE FLOWER
SHROUD OF ROSES
SKULL GARDEN

The Blair and Piermont Crime Thriller Series:

(with Donna Warner)
TARGETED
DEATH'S FOOTPRINT

ABOUT THE AUTHOR

Formerly a procedure writer/ editor at a nuclear power plant, Gloria Ferris is the award-winning author of the humorous Cornwall & Redfern mystery series. She also writes the Blair and Piermont thriller suspense series with co-author, Donna Warner. Blood Shield is the second Young Adult Fantasy book in the BLOOD series. Occasionally, Gloria will write a short story just for the heck of it and is currently working on an Adult Paranormal Urban Fantasy novel. When she isn't writing, she watches how-to webinars, researches poisons and weapons, and is often heard to mutter, "I wish I'd written that!" She lives in southwestern Ontario and has a dog now but still wants a monkey.

NOTE FROM THE AUTHOR

I hope you enjoyed reading BLOOD SHIELD. If you did, please consider leaving a review on the vendor site where you purchased this book. Authors live for reviews, and even a few words make us so happy!